Chasing Pillows

William Cooper

Chasing Pillows

AEON ENTERPRISES, INC., MARCH 2014

www.AeonEnt.com

Cover illustration and book design by
Aeon Enterprises, Inc.

ISBN — 978-0-9886275-6-7
V1.0_r1

Printed in U.S.A.

Chapter One

The following texts are a compilation of my friend's writings. They contain descriptions of his dispositions and an insight into his thoughts. His name is Opaulde and he begins where my name ends.

—Darcy

EVIL.

That's what I am.

I see little children abusing things they see as alien.

I see girls gossiping and being cruel.

I see boys being rowdy and foolish.

HATE.

That is what I feel.

A burning rage, insatiable by anything less than death.

But the death of others?

Or the death of myself?

EMBITTERED.

That's what I am. That is what I feel.

When I realise everything that is wrong with the world exists within me as well.

When I realise my hate is more about me than anyone else.

I hate in others what I don't want to accept in myself.

If what I see as evil is me and it is everywhere, what is good?

WHEN I WAS YOUNGER THERE was no question in my mind as to who I was. Because as far as I was aware, I was all that was. The thoughts that sprout from the minds of children, to them, are the very most fundamental features of the world in its entirety. But as time goes on, we discover that there are other ... things ... that share our world with us and in time we stop thinking of it as our world and begin to call it the world.

Sure, we have our inner world that we consider private to ourselves and perhaps a few intimate individuals, but for the most part we are aware that a world exists that consists of more than ourselves. So in time the question arises that causes us to ask ourselves who we are in this world. Or maybe I'm making assumptions; we do tend to do that, don't we? We assume that a major component of our lives and the lives around us simply must be present for everyone else as well. It could be this concept of we, where the world we live in begins to consist of ourselves amongst others. We compare ourselves to them and we judge accordingly.

I can't remember if the questions had started at this point. Whether or not the *Voices* had begun their great chanting inquiry. All I recall is the story I had read of a girl that was robbed of what most of us consider as basic rights.

The girl who was called Genie had been abused from her early life to her prepubescent years. Bound for much of this time and restricted to a single room, she was almost entirely cut off from socialisation, and consequently the fundamental psychological growth of childhood, and suffered from malnutrition and physical defects.

I can't remember if this opened my mind to the dynamic nature of life, but looking back on it now, it does. I wanted to read over it again; I was shocked at the time, I hadn't quite heard of anything on this scale before. We hear about deaths every day, but this affected me deeply. I don't know why, and perhaps I never will. I never had the chance to read the story again because I was quickly drawn back into the chaotic and deceivingly pointless life of a human being.

I was late for school. Yes, I was a student; please restrain your awe at such a unique and original concept. I won't bore you with the details of a trip to school, nor the name of said institution or the colours of the cars travelling down the opposite side of the road. Not because I don't think that's an excellent form of storytelling, but because I can't remember. For it was not only a very long time ago, but my mind was set on something else: a girl. That's right; a female specimen.

At the time I was not aware of how stereotypical this was because I was so deeply screwed into the emotional state I had found myself in. My heart rate increased with every metre I neared the school and I was sweating. How no one else in the vehicle noticed this I can only assume was due to their own busy, chaotic and pointless thoughts. But I must apologise, for I have made you misunderstand a certain point. It's not that these thoughts are pointless; on the contrary, I'm sure that the thought "I have to hurry up, dancing class is in fifteen minutes!" has a point to it ... but does it have that other thing ... the thing that we define beyond the worded definition ... does it have meaning?

Well, I certainly thought my thought had meaning. We came into the school car park, we said our usual farewells, and I departed the vehicle. What wasn't usual was what I planned to do. Instead of heading to class I walked along the outer fence of the college and waited. I waited for her to arrive. My heart was beating heavily, but it was destined to beat with even more ferocity than I knew was possible.

She exited her vehicle and I watched in my peripheral as she walked up the stairs and into my general direction.

I played the moments to come through my mind for what must have been the millionth time. Wait until she gets within two metres ... turn to her ... verbalise the words, "Hello Blair"... (ensure casual undertones with the right hint of enthusiasm) ... wait for response ... ask, "How are you today?"... if she responds with warmth ask, "Did you sleep well?"

This didn't happen. She slowed down when she was within two metres of me. I thought to myself, "Okay, okay. Wait until one metre ..." And when she was behind me I thought the same thing, and gradually two metres became chasing her and yelling "Blair!"

Except that didn't happen either. I was left standing there, my heart slowing but the stress remaining ... slumping down into my stomach where it mocked me and stroked my heartache. But something snapped. This was at least the tenth time that I was unable to speak to her and my mind couldn't take it anymore. The consistent inability to accomplish something that is required for what you feel is the most important thing that you could do in your life becomes, at a certain point, unacceptable. I ran up into the classroom and with a red face that showed all of my facial flaws I shouted her name. Compression and rarefaction transmitted the word across the room ... and I felt it move across every particle of air ... because in the same moment Blair's lips locked with a boy's. The tallest. The fastest. The strongest boy in the school. My voice hit their mouths like an irritating smell. For a moment, I think they may have considered ignoring it. But eventually, with their lips still together, Blair's eyes shifted over to mine. There was no warmth there, just a glare of alienation and mild confusion as to why this thing in front of her was saying her name. And when their lips parted, so did the two halves of my heart.

The figure's hands were steady as he aimed with perfect accuracy towards the animal. He released his grip and the arrow flew with immeasurable power.

I can't know if you are or are not aware of the dedication a person can make to the feelings they have for another person. Some of the greatest historical and literary tales in human knowledge are based around love, especially of an obsessive nature: Romeo and Juliet, in which the love-struck pair known as Romeo and Juliet kill themselves as a preferable option to living without each other.

Love is everywhere, consisting of different elements. Sometimes it comes in the form of a purely sexual nature. Other depictions include bonding of other kinds: romantic dinner dates and adventurous tales. But no matter what breed of the concept of love it is, it can be found almost everywhere in the world. It is fundamental to human survival—relationships and reproduction. The binding factor in the concept of we that we begin to be drawn into as we mature.

I wondered, because Genie never developed in these ways, she knew nothing but fear and pain, whether I should just have been grateful to simply have these feelings for another person. The pain I felt for Blair would not even account for the smallest fraction of Genie's suffering ... so surely, in perspective, the happiness that these feelings for Blair brought to me was something I should have been grateful for, despite the pain that came with it.

I was damaged from what had happened that day at school. But I kept going. I continued on the path of trying to get closer to her, and especially, express my affections for her. At some point—I think it was during a conversation with one of her friends—I got the idea in my head that a love letter was my last chance and so I spent the next few months writing. I recall scrapping everything and restarting many times. In the end, I came up with this:

Blair,

A lifetime will pass before I can fully express my feelings for you.

Your smile is imprinted on my mind, and the very thought of you brightens up even my loneliest of nights.

Just to see you, your hair, eyes and face, is enough to make me happy.

The words of this world are not meaningful enough to answer the beauty I see in you.

You are that one girl, in all of the world, that means the most to me.

The funniest, sweetest, and overall most brilliant and amazing girl I have ever met.

You are kindhearted, and an incredibly stunning person.

But all of this is summed up by three words, that I hope I may one day say freely.

Deepest of affections.

Always,

Opaulde

I sent the letter. I had to hide its existence under a number of lies. First, to my parents, the lie was that I was sending a secret message to my friends. To my uncle, who caught me in action as he drove by, I said that it was in response to a school notice that had been sent home to me as a result of my impressive grades. Everyone believed. What reason did they have not to? In my life I was a trustworthy person. Unlike some people, that seem to struggle through their lives, grasping whatever they can get their hands on and harming anyone in their way. Perhaps those people, in a similar, but different way, are like Genie when compared to me.

They don't have the environment needed to be trustworthy. They are what they are because of their circumstances. Like all of us. Genie could not feel love because she had not learnt to. We all have different places inside the we in our lives. Different statuses within society.

Some of us spend our whole lives trying to rise up through them, while others accept them for what they are. These things, too, seem to be decided by how we perceive ourselves within we. Is that what it was all about? My obsession with Blair could have just been my attempt to raise my own position in society. Are all actions just that; a way to increase your standing in something? As I envisioned it, the letter arrived. Blair received it, loved it, fell in love with me, we got married at the age of twenty and moved to Spain where we had three children named Mick, Ben and Laura. The end.

That may have been what I had expected to happen, somewhere in my twisted mind. So I was surprised when at school the next week, everyone had read it, and I was to be forever known as the twit that wrote a love letter for the alpha jock's girlfriend. Because there's nothing a person likes to do more than make fun of someone lower on the social hierarchy.

Despite the intention, do you not think that when someone in a privileged country "likes" an image on Facebook that claims to support help for impoverished communities, that they would be insulted? Insulted by the hollow compassion sent out to them that contains no weight or real impact? But surely there are people that do make a real difference ... but they seem to be a minority. I wonder where they come from. Also ... how can one tell the difference between one who is genuine, and one that deceives?

The alpha jock came up to me one day and said, "Hey, you, ya funny. You can hang with us if you want to."

Being a fool at the time, I responded, "Oh, yeah! Sure!"

Thus something worse than outright bullying began to happen. I would sit with their group every day at school, and they allowed me to contribute in anything they did, no matter how bad I was at it. It was all as you would expect a friendship group to be. Except people were suspicious about it. Unfortunately, at the time, I was not.

My teacher called me over one day, and spoke to me in a hushed tone: "Opaulde, are you aware that they only include you to make fun of you?"

I stood there, thinking about something I had not even considered. But it did make sense, if I actually did consider it. Every time I would stare at Blair, there would be laughs. Every time I said something wrong in class, there would be laughs. If I couldn't even manage to kick the football—laughs. Yes, it was true, I was only in the group as an amusement to them. A runt that wasn't necessary but was kept all the same. Which is where I think humans can be far more ferocious in their ways than other animals. A runt in nature simply dies. It no longer exists.

There is no need in other species for a weak element to be mocked and kept around as an amusement. In some species, the group is only considered as strong as its weakest. In a strange way, this makes the weakest member the most important. Perhaps that's where the human minority comes from: the strand of psychology that asks us to help the weakest for the strength of everyone as a united community.

When someone like Genie is discovered, she is helped. There is a compassion amongst our many emotions. Yet what happened to her was done by her father, also a human, and so there is great cruelty within our emotions as well. But it was not here that I realised the great dynamic of life. Something more personal to me would have to happen before my eyes were opened completely.

At first I did nothing about it. I allowed them to see me as their joke and I didn't particularly mind. Somewhere in my head it was my only way to get closer to Blair. She did speak to me now, and something about her tone made me believe that she didn't like to make fun of me like the others. Somewhere in her was something good. Because surely if there was not, I never would have fallen in love with her in the first place.

Things continued in a consistent fashion until one day when I found myself amongst a fight that had started from within the group. The alpha jock's strength was being challenged by a slightly more muscular boy.

They brawled for a fair five minutes without stopping to breathe. Someone from behind me, I think it was the troublemaker of the group, decided it would be amusing to push me into the fray. I wasn't aware of much after that, because I was thrown to the ground and as far as I can tell was not conscious again for quite some time.

I WOKE UP IN THE hospital. I didn't feel any pain, and for some reason I felt that this was an important point to make so I said, "I don't feel any pain."

A doctor who was in the room watching over my condition replied, "You will once the shock wears off, unfortunately. Try to get some rest. But before you do, your mother is waiting outside. Would you like me to call to her?"

I considered this for a moment. My mother. The woman that birthed me. The one that taught me how to express many of the emotions that I have the potential to feel. But not all people have a mother. And some have one that doesn't freely give her love. Why would a mother not give her child love? There may be many reasons, but what of the particular reason that is she is unable to?

Genie's mother didn't want her daughter to be abused like she was. It was the dominance and instability of the father figure that made it impossible for her mother to do anything. Yet in the end, it was her mother that saved her from the household. That motherly love saved Genie's life. One does not feel content in imagining what state she would have gone on to be in, if she had survived for much longer.

Yes, this was what a mother was to me. When I heard the word "mother" I pictured a status within the we of my life that was caring, loving and comforting.

"Yes," I said.

Many young people resent their parents. The people that give them food, clothing and shelter. Why? Is it a natural method of gaining independence? Emotional dispositions lead us to have children. Sometimes it happens in accidental passion. Reproduction is everywhere. Despite the confronting number of deaths that occur worldwide every minute, the population still manages to increase. We are programmed for it. It is all we know. There are those who turn against it. But once again, they are a minority, and occur only in the most extreme of emotional states.

I once heard of a religion that contained a core belief that reproduction was not to happen. This made me laugh because a religion is the result of the spread of beliefs, and society is the result of a spread of reproduction. To have one without the other is a very rare thing indeed. I do believe that if that particular religion has not been lost to the world by now, it will be very soon. I don't know how they answered the question "Who am I?" with "Something that shouldn't reproduce", but at some point for some reason they must have come to believe that that's who they were in the world.

In the same way that I was now beginning to see that I was a lesser being in the world. No one wanted me for me, they wanted me for what they could do to me. Was I a good person to my mother or just something to pour her love into? I felt useless. I had no place in the world. But in this I also found motivation. If I wasn't good enough for Blair, I would become good enough for Blair, no matter what it would take. I would prove them all wrong. I would become stronger and faster, I would do my very best to grow taller. I would not stop until Blair wanted me like I wanted her. I would rather die than give in.

"Fight through the pain!" I screamed at myself, faking a strength in tone that my body could not. And no matter how daunting the road ahead was, I had my motivation. I had Blair in my mind. The goal was set, and all I had to do was step up and accomplish it.

T HE SENSATION OF GUSHING WATER against my body must have woken me. I don't remember falling asleep ... or had I been knocked unconscious? I don't know. I could feel blood pouring from my nose, dissolving into the liquid around me. Where was I? This was the first time one of my voices took control of my perception. I was in a dark room. It was completely dark except for a single dot of light in front of me. I counted; it changed colour in a timing of about five seconds.

A voice appeared in my mind and asked for my name. By some instinct I responded that my name was Esteban Julio Ricardo Montoya De la Rosa Ramirez. I felt a burning sensation as I felt the *Voice* slap me, but I could not work out how. In some way, my response was to slap it back. I felt my hand making contact with the *Voice* but when I looked at it, it had not moved. Yet it was red like when a hand has been recently slapped against something.

The *Voice* bellowed in my mind, "WHO ARE YOU? WHO ARE YOU? WHO ARE YOU?"

I panicked for a response, knowing that somewhere, somehow, I was slowly bleeding and wouldn't survive for much longer. Was I submerged? I responded with the words that came to me. They felt unnatural and alien but it was as if I had no choice. "I ... Hannah Montana ... am in fact ... Miley Cyrus."

The *Voice* began to growl like a hurricane; everything that was standing still simply ceased to be, but not before flipping in multiple directions at once. Could I feel myself spinning in deep water? Was this my mind's way of comprehending my end? The floor fell apart, disappearing without a trace. I fell. But it was as if I was falling into the sky. I could feel my lungs filling with water. Through no laws of nature I was able to yell out into the cold that was engulfing me, "HELP ME!"

There was no response, just a silence that is what I had imagined panic would sound like if such silence had a sound. Life left my body. I felt a cold so frozen that warmth seemed an impossible concept. Like when Blair's lips locked with another boy's. Like when that little girl I read about not two weeks ago was locked in her room for a decade. What was love to that little girl? Nothing. Love did not exist to her. Warmth did not exist to me. Not the warmth of my body nor the warmth of Blair's lips. Yet I would give up the former for just a few moments of the latter.

An object appeared in front of me. What was this? I stared closer. How could an object exist ... wherever I was? I didn't know, and for some reason I didn't care. I simply reached out and grabbed the object. Some purpose lay within its presence. I brought it closer. Chocolate. It was chocolate. Again, by some instinct, I offered the *Voice*, which I had no way of knowing was still there, the chocolate. I don't know if it accepted it.

But I do know I appeared on a beach. That's a very nice thing to affiliate yourself with, sure. I thought the same thing. But soon I realised that with the clashing of the waves against the shore, I felt my body weaken, my senses fail. I looked out into the great depths of this seemingly endless body of water. I could see myself. A great light was fixed on my body, judging me.

"But I have tried so hard. Who are you to judge me?" I asked the silence.

"WHO ARE YOU?" the *Voice* in my mind asked, as the water began to boil and the sand began to move beneath my feet. "WHO? WHO? WHO?" The *Voice* grew louder, no longer a question but a demand for a worthy response.

The water was gone now; it had boiled away, as if it never was. The sand came together into great clumps until it became one great stone. The ground moved until what had been a beach was now a mountain.

"WHO ARE YOU? WHO WERE YOU? WHO ... WILL ... YOU ... BE?" The *Voice* was losing its composure.

I listened as the same words repeated, again and again. Each time the words were weaker, as if the lungs of the *Voice* were slowly being blocked. The *Voice* had lungs? I didn't understand. I do now. But I didn't then. My mind was too shrouded. I didn't know what the *Voice* was.

I didn't understand as I felt the *Voice* plummeting into the depths of a distant body of water. I stood on the mountain that had grown from the past and I listened ... tasted ... saw ... as the *Voice* slowly ebbed away to nothing. I saw my life ... my birth, my education, my friendships, my victories and my losses.

"What does it all account for ...?" the *Voice* muttered.

I saw Blair. I recalled the recent time that I yelled her name across the classroom and her only response was a glance of confusion. I recalled when the laughs of dozens of people hit my back, my face ... from all directions.

"Who ... are ... we?" asked the *Voice*.

"I DON'T KNOW!" I shouted back.

I HAD NEVER BEEN WHAT convention described as normal. Ever since I was very young I did things in ways that other children didn't. In subtle ways at first: I would talk to my toys and they would talk to each other, but that is just the play of a creative mind, right?

There was also a darker side to my playing: toys would be found hanging from ropes in a way that assumed suicide ... or murder. Yes, I was an interesting child but things got worse.

First the anxiety appeared when I couldn't be left alone with people I didn't know. But that was just a child being shy, surely. It seems we do that with everything, don't we? We justify it all, even the things that we had not wanted to happen. Like a goal that slowly consumes all morals, we dedicate ourselves more and more to a cause.

Adolf Hitler's attempts to give rebirth to the glory of the German nation, leading to the holocaust of millions of Jewish people. Am I supposed to believe that he wanted that? Perhaps he was that twisted. Or had it just become a necessary wall between him and his ever-demanding goal?

We decide in our minds that with the accomplishment of these goals, we will be the perfect me. We will become the ultimate version of ourselves. I didn't have these goals when I was young. Children, more often than adults, find happiness in a lack of goals—freedom. Life seems to be a spontaneous adventure from the eyes of a child.

I recall the joys of simply playing in a tree. Everything was magical. I never doubted the existence of magic because truth wasn't a concept in my mind. Anything was possible. Then the chains of logic and reason came in. They flood childhood like a river, and with the assistance of these goals, all happiness and joy that came simply from life itself ... slowly ebb away.

I ask myself now, even if I had accomplished what I wanted, would I be happy? Was Blair really someone that I could see myself living the rest of my life with? But I didn't consider otherwise at the time. Because the emotions I felt for her had clouded my mind. And even now I speak about my emotions as if they are superior to the ones I once had. But how superior are they really? And what would it take ... what little amount of change would it take for me to change my mind again? How easily do our perceptions of who we are change?

When I was in my early teen years, I considered myself above love. Such a thing was for lesser humans who couldn't understand that love was nothing more than a chemical process. Yet at this point in my story I stand as an example of the one thing I claimed I would never become. How often does this happen? How many of us recall saying to a loved one or friend that we would never change; that we would always be loyal or kind or a shoulder to lean on? Time destroys that. Time destroys our perception of who we are. Like when maturity crushes the spontaneity and simplicity that is the beauty of childhood.

I believed that Blair would save me from this. I saw her as something that I could bury myself into and rise again as that spontaneous creature that I once was. And in my mind, we would be as such together. Untouched by the pain I began to feel in the absence of it. And thus I started to miss something I had never had. That I didn't, if I was to be honest with myself, even know existed.

I WAS STANDING IN FRONT of my house, holding a towel under my arm. I had planned to go to the beach. It was a freezing cold day but I was determined to go swimming, which is excellent for fitness, which I needed to get Blair's attention.

While the alpha jock was muscular, his most prominent attribute was his speed. He could run across the school in record time. Fast enough to not lose his place in a conversation if the nature of it was broad enough. Perhaps that's an exaggeration, but exaggerations are how people remember things. And what people remember is more important than what is. What is becomes important when it is the only thing that can be changed to manipulate what people remember. So I was heading for the beach.

But where had those earlier thoughts come from? My mind scanned for a reasonable connection to the ... thoughts of drowning ... and the *Voice*. Had my mother warned me to be careful? Yes. Yes that must have been it. My worry-sick mother had been afraid that I wouldn't be okay in the harsh weather. That's exactly what had happened.

WE WERE ALL SITTING IN a circle. Blair was opposite me. I was staring, as usual. Why did I stare? Was it my only way to try to find a connection that didn't exist? I pondered this, but was woken from a daydream by the absence of anyone else in the room other than myself and

Blair. There was an awkwardness. We were alone. I tried to think of something to say. She was smiling in the way people smile when they try to hide awkwardness.

I decided to ask a question. It was a terrible choice of question. "If I was more attractive would you like me?"

But there was no response from her. Just the laughs of all of her friends as they appeared in the room again. The alpha jock carried a camera in his hands, and laughed the loudest of all of them.

I didn't tell my parents. Not because they wouldn't understand or anything like that. But they were both strong people, and I didn't want to show myself to them with weakness. And maybe I was shy. I have never had great public success with love. The longer you are unsuccessful, the less confident you can become. You question yourself and who you are.

I walked into my home and sat down at the kitchen table. My mother asked me how my day was but I had no energy left with which to respond so I remained silent. Why do people ask if you're okay when you look as if you're not? Do they think that someone in distress would want a person to blatantly trip into their moody aura? But I'm being cynical. Maybe she just wanted to help. But I didn't consider that at the time.

I snapped at her and she responded with, "You can't be like this ... dinner is in fifteen!" in a way that promised but couldn't deliver on a lecture.

I ate, but I ate little, only as much as I needed to not be hungry. We don't often do that in our culture, do we? Or do we? I don't know. I didn't know anymore and I didn't care anymore. All I wanted was to die. I had become useless. My way of gaining status in my own little mental world map had been eradicated. And all the rest of the world could do was laugh.

I lay on my bed and stared at the ceiling. I didn't want the world to continue. From this point onward there was nothing in my future but pain. I couldn't see any way out. Even if there was a way out of it, I didn't want it. I wanted Blair. You can say as many times as you like to a heartbroken person that there are "plenty of fish in the ocean" but it doesn't matter. The truth didn't matter to me because in my pocket fantasy there was only one thing that could bring me happiness.

Why did the words keep going? Why couldn't my thoughts have just stopped there? It would have been better … no, not better … it would have been … nothing. Nothing was what I wanted. I blamed myself. Not just my actions but the entirety of my being.

I grabbed my own body and tried to hit myself. Some hits, I knew, would cause bruises. That's what I wanted. Because I was unworthy. Do you know what it's like to be abandoned by your own mind? Maybe you do.

Doesn't anyone that has felt grief? Because isn't that all a simulation in our brains? A betrayal of everything around us! Our lives, our thoughts, our very environment turns its back on us and we are left with one simple desire. The desire to no longer exist. Because it is existence that brought these emotions upon us. Existence is what you blame when there's nothing left to blame but yourself.

It didn't burn at this point. The flame inside my mind that was tearing me apart temporarily stopped and I was left with a feeling of emptiness. I was lost inside myself.

Only one thought remained as I examined the knife in my hands: I needed to be punished. One final goal was left to be achieved. It was the only thing left in my power and like a slave drawn to a sacred text I followed it and I only stopped short of the barrier that is survival. I liked it; the conflict between duty and survival.

Survival always puts in a persistent struggle. But responsibility to my new goal was getting stronger, too. It may have been young, but I knew it would grow, with time. Perhaps eventually ... eventually ... I would succeed in ending it. My final happiness. Or would I feel fear? There it is again: survival—striking back the desire for death.

The survival of poor little Genie's body as it clung to life for so long and the duty of her mother to save her that overcame the fear of her husband. That is who she was, and this ... this is who I was. I was my own demise.

DINNER WAS DULL. THE FLAVOURS lacked meaning. Everything lacked meaning. The thoughts that had been so meaningful to me were now the reason for everything else lacking meaning. I took mouthful after mouthful, swallowing at the earliest convenience but never enjoying the textures.

My mother was concerned because it was my favourite dish—agnolotti. Usually a dish that excited me immensely. What's more, I hadn't had it in a very long time. I told her I was feeling sick. And wasn't I? People take that response as meaning biological sickness but never question whether it could in fact be a psychological issue.

Sometimes a psychological issue is the very cause of disease. Depression can lead to bad posture which leads to misalignment of the spine leading to almost all possible health problems. But I didn't care. I wanted health problems. That sort of mindset is criticised widely. But it was who I was. The boy who was sick who wanted to die. Because what was life without the hope of Blair? I was sick without her, and that's exactly what I told her. I sent her a message that very night saying just that.

She replied with, "K."

"Forgive me?" I asked.

"For what?"

"Being weird."

"Oh k."

There was a pause because I couldn't think of what to say next.

"You are beautiful."

"Oh, k, thanks," was her reply.

"I love you."

There was no reply, so I sent another message. "I really do." After another twenty minutes. "So, so, so, so much!" But there was no reply. I hadn't quite gotten the hint. I waited until early in the morning when I involuntarily fell asleep. Maybe she lost her phone, I told myself. I'm almost certain these days that she hadn't.

When one comfort drains away, the mind has an incredible way of finding comfort in something else. Food was my most common secondary pleasure. There are so many different options! First, I started simple: I made myself some pesto toast with mushrooms. It was delicious. But I'm not one to stop at so little. I boiled some eggs, made up some more pesto toast (because who can get enough pesto) and salted them all over (I have a salt deficiency and therefore love salt). I made some pancakes and once I had perfected them I made some bacon and polished it off quickly.

I sat in front of the television. The device that controls lives everywhere in the developed world. The neighbours' dog barked in the background. I was home alone. I checked the pantry and fridge for more food but there wasn't any. I was disappointed.

I thought of Genie, lying hungry and alone. Here I was, perfectly full, wanting more and more. Gluttony ... no matter how justified in anyone's mind is gluttony. We are omnivores, possessing the potential ferocity and cruelty of a carnivore and the potential peace of herbivore communities. We are the most complex society of animals that we know of. Yet everything we do boils down to simplicity. Everything can be generalised into fundamental categories of life.

I didn't want that to be true. And Blair made me feel like it wasn't. With her around, the world was a magical place. When she failed me, there was food. But then food, too, failed me when I looked in the mirror and saw my health deteriorate. When that happened, I felt Blair get further and further away from my future. The body lets that happen to itself, doesn't it? Allows pleasure to lead to obesity and illness. There are great flaws in nature. But then again, flaws are—

There was a knock at the door. I went to open it and standing in the doorway was Blair. I yelped. It wasn't actually her; it was my mother. "Oh, Mother."

"Hey darling."

"Where have you been?" I asked.

"Out."

"Right." I wandered up into my room because I didn't really have anything to say to her. So now that the temporary pleasures of food had worn off, I just lay there, and despaired.

Another flaw, perhaps, that the mind lingers on things in unproductive ways. Or perhaps it is simply the result of losing the need for survival. Becoming so dependent on the state of your environment that you become complacent and weak thus aren't able to deal with any issues that come your way. I didn't really care. Laziness. Laziness. So powerful. Like a conscious sleep it drains everything ... even my words now. Feel its power. Tick.

You didn't read them all, did you? Why? Because they are all the same? If that is the case then is the only thing that keeps you reading the contrast of a word to the words that follow it? Or the meaning you gain from that contrast? Meaning. What meaning do you get from these words? 'There was a carrot in the under gym of the keyboard.' Is there meaning in that? If not, why not? If there is ... if there was ... if there will be ...

Perhaps you did read them all. In that case, ask yourself why. Because my tale must continue.

I WOKE UP. I DIDN'T remember falling asleep. It scared me. I got up; my head was burning from confusion. What time was it? I ran down the stairs. Someone was in the kitchen.

"What have you done to me?"

I didn't hear a response. I grabbed a knife to defend myself. Any movement, I swiped at.

"What have you done to my head?"

I could hear sounds, but I couldn't distinguish them from the beating of my skull. Or could I not distinguish the beating of my skull from sounds? I ran for what I thought was the door but slammed into what must have been a wall. I tried again, this time tripping on something that I couldn't identify. As I fell the knife in my hand slashed my leg and I felt myself bleeding. Hands grabbed at me as I screamed and thrashed. Millions of arms were lashing out at me.

I WOKE UP AGAIN. I was still on my bed. My television was on and a blue creature was yapping about biscuits ... or maybe it was cookies. I went downstairs, this time with a cleared mind. The knife I had grabbed was in the same place it had been before I had grabbed it. My mother was in the kitchen.

"Mum, did something just happen?"

"Did what happen, hun?"

"I ... don't know ..." I went back up to my room.

Had I dreamt it? Yes, I must have. Weird dreams happen, it's nothing to be concerned about. I thought back to the dream I had had when I was younger. I was being stalked by a man in my school. He caught me and stabbed me with a syringe. When I woke up, I could feel a pain in my back. Just a creation of the mind, nothing real about it whatsoever.

My leg was itching. The same thing was happening, my mind making up pains that weren't there. I laughed, how ridiculous. I scratched my leg. Then I brought my hand to my face to scratch my itchy chin as well. It was covered in blood.

Do you ever look at life and realise it has no meaning? In particular, your life. You spend weeks, months, sometimes even years pining over something and then you just realise that it is meaningless. You feel stupid. This is how I began to feel. Because in all reality, my feelings for Blair were probably stupid. The way I hurt myself for them was probably stupid. And the way I imagined that anything I felt really mattered at all was probably stupid.

I walked past Blair; this time, I didn't look at her like I always did. I just kept walking. She didn't notice. Why should she have? If I left everyone alone, would anyone notice at all? If I suddenly stopped engaging, stopped making an effort, would I find that no one was making an effort for me? Did I want that or not? Of course not, I didn't want to be alone. Or maybe I wanted not to not to want to be alone. Or did I want to not not want to not be alone. I don't think I even knew. I was reacting on instinct and emotion.

My school work quality disintegrated, as far as I thought, and so when report day came, I was predicting terrible results. I always got pretty good grades; they weren't brilliant, but just as good as anyone else's. As the reports were being handed out I dreamt of leaving. It occurred to me why people must love and desire holidays so much. Because you change your environment. When your environment changes, the expectations of who you are can change. I pictured a new world. One that was happy and peaceful. I ran through fields and ate whatever I wanted whenever I wanted to. Blair was there and she was with me every day and every night. We ate together, we played and talked together. We touched. Everything was ... perfect.

Was perfection what I wanted? I don't know. It didn't matter anymore. None of it did. Not even my pain mattered; I was a shadow. It felt as if there was nothing left to me. Like I had been left out in a harsh storm that had torn my soul from my body. My mind. My one, single mind always had lots of thoughts. About many things. They were all gone now. All I had left was an emptiness that was impossible to escape. I think, in a way, the emptiness was me; I was the emptiness. I was empty. The words you are reading now ... is there anything in them? Are they empty too? Who are you? Who do you think I am? Who do you think you are? Maybe you matter. All I knew was that I didn't.

As I watched my fellow classmates wait for their reports I ... chocolate, rainbow, pigeon, waffle ... couldn't help but realise that their minds were ... fluffy pillows and soft pink cake ... on their own reports, not mine. They would never care what my results were; why should they? I didn't matter ... a nice warm fire spitting ash into the air ... I just wanted to go home, now ... the smell of light burning and food cooking ... where I could eat, get fat and not have to think about anything else ... Blair. Blair's report was handed to her. Did she care what her results were? I wondered. I wondered other things in that moment too. Who was Blair? And how could I believe that she was meant for me if I didn't know that ... and didn't know who I was, either? It burnt.

I felt an involuntary pulse move through my body. I yelped and everyone looked at me. "I'll live," I said, and everyone went back to their waiting or various acts of stupidity. Did they all matter? They all mattered to someone. I didn't. But I did. I mattered to my mother. I mattered to most of my family. But I wanted to matter to Blair. But why her? Who was she to me? I couldn't answer the questions. I thought I could.

I remember when I first began to have feelings for her. She was the thing that gave everything meaning. And now she was the thing that was taking it away. I recall saying to myself that she was my purpose. The one thing in all of the world that could make my life whole. Was I looking for a purpose? I couldn't remember the time before her or what was in my mind. Had I forgotten who I was? Is a purpose real if who you are becomes the purpose itself? If the only defining factor of my life, to me, is her ... who am I? And if I don't know who she is ... who are we? Who is anyone?

I looked at everyone in the room. Each doing something different to pass the time before school ended. I had received my report and it was laying on my desk. What was their purpose? Did they need one? Did they feel they needed one? Surely someone else asks these questions ... or does everyone else just ... be? Never actually asking that question, "Who am I?" No. No, I don't believe that's true. Surely we all ask. We may all look for different things when asking the question but surely we all wonder who we are in the world. But looking from the outside, I couldn't see any defining factors. There were no Leonardo da Vincis in the room. Or was there? How does one know when someone is special? These questions were diluting my mind and leading me to question my own persona once again. I remembered that I had decided that it didn't matter. Because I wasn't a Leonardo da Vinci, I didn't matter. That's all I needed to know. That is who I was, as far as I was concerned. In some strange way I had found what I had wanted: an identity. When asked who I was, I could now quite happily respond with something I was finally confident in. "I am someone who doesn't matter."

But I can make myself matter. I was lying on my back with weights in either arm. I raised my arms into the air, still holding them, and I held them there. My arms started to burn. I ignored it. "Be strong," I whispered to myself through gritted teeth. Eventually, obviously, I became incapable of holding them there. "Why does this have to be so slow?" I yelled at no one. I screamed.

I lifted a weight and considered throwing it but stopped myself when I realised that it possibly wasn't a good idea. "What now?" I asked myself. I knew that if I was going to do this there were two things that were more important than anything else: cardiovascular endurance and strength. If I could increase those, everything else should fall into place, I thought.

I used the weights in every way I could come up with until I was too sore to lift them at all. I went to get a drink and ended up sculling a litre of water. Because water increases the loss of fat, I thought, as I felt my stomach, seeming to be eternally covered in a beautiful layer of lard. I would make a good fatty oil, I thought to myself. These thoughts angered me.

I got the biggest backpack I could find and piled as many weights into it as I could manage. I included some heavy books for safe measure. I weighed it and it was thirty kilograms. That increased my weight to about one hundred and ten kilograms. That would increase the number of calories I burnt by a good margin, but only if I gave my body a reason to do so. This was good, because it was working my strength. But I wasn't going to stop at just that.

I got onto the treadmill and set it up. I began to walk. That way my heart would get going too. I set the timer for three hours. At the speed I was going at, I would get about twenty kilometres in that time. That sounded good. Surely that would benefit me. The first hour was easy, I was motivated. The second hour was more of an issue. I tried to distract myself. First by using the television, but when that failed, I had nothing but Blair in my mind. She kept me going. I don't know why, but the thought of her pushed me onwards.

The third hour wasn't something I could distract my mind from. By now the straps of the backpack were digging into me so much that I could feel pressure on my organs. I felt all of the pain. There were no distractions. But I kept stepping. My mind focused on each step like it was the last. I promised myself that this was the only way out of it. My mind trusted me. And in turn my body trusted me. Like a young child it did what its superior said was best. I had conquered myself. There were only a few metres left. I told myself that I was so close. Was it a minute left? I couldn't tell because my eyes were blinded by my own tears. But by the way the treadmill beeped I knew I was close. It beeps every minute. I had counted every single one. One hundred and seventy nine beeps, I had counted. And then it beeped again. I almost couldn't believe that it was going to end. I had, at some point, accepted that this was what I was doing.

My body set itself into a rhythmic pattern. It was in survival mode. And that's exactly where I wanted it to be. But had I pushed myself too far? This final minute felt like a year. Every second was a two-hour examination. Now knowing that it didn't have long to go, my body was paddling to the finish line. "Help," I yelped through my own sweat. "Help. Me."

Like something more than coincidence, in that moment my phone received a message from Blair. 'Blair', it said on the screen, flashing, and the first sentence of the message was there too, but too small for my mind to process in that condition. The flash of Blair's existence was enough to push me through the next few seconds with fury. I screamed now, ignoring any formation or dignity. I started to jog each step instead of walking them. When I did this, I could feel the blisters that had formed along the impact points of my feet.

I looked at my feet, curious as to whether they were still whole. They were. But there was blood. I hadn't noticed, but my socks were soaked in blood. I panicked. How long had my feet been bleeding? How much blood had I lost? An inner anxiety took over. A *Voice* in my head started to see blood everywhere. It spilt out of me onto the floor. "I'm dying!" my mouth said. But it wasn't me who was speaking. This *Voice* took over my entire mind.

If I was bleeding, how I could I protect Blair? Was Blair okay? I didn't feel the pain anymore. But what it was replaced by was far worse than any physical pain. I feared for Blair. How could I make sure she was safe when I wasn't allowed to be with her? "Let me keep you safe!" The *Voice* yelled out.

It was because I was too weak. I wasn't strong enough for her. Too weak! Too weak! Fifteen seconds. Too weak! Fourteen seconds. I needed to be stronger. I needed to keep going ... For Blair. Ten seconds. I needed to! Nine seconds. I pulled the backpack further up onto my shoulders and I pushed my muscles in a general forward direction. Six seconds. "Blair! Blair! Blair!" Four seconds. My mind was in a flurry of spastic energy. "I will be strong enough for you ..." Two seconds. I reached forward to reset the timer for another hour. I missed the button and fell forward. The full force of the backpack pushed me downward and I was knocked unconscious against the treadmill.

What happened next was very quick, as contrast usually is. We wait for weeks and months and years for something and then it comes and goes in seconds.

"I like you," Blair said to me one day when I got to school.

I had no words. Something did come out, though it was far from what I should have said. "Oharrgh."

"You're really sweet and funny and I'm really sorry for everything I've sort of put you through. I realise that he was a jerk but I want now to sort of be with you because you're really nice and I think you actually really love me for me because otherwise you wouldn't have waited all of this time for me."

It had been two years since I yelled her name across the classroom. She was right. I had waited for a very long time. But now that the moment came for me to do something about it, my confidence had withered away to nothing. I had been left alone with no one but myself for so long now that it had destroyed something essential inside. I knew I would never be the same again.

"Why?" I managed to blurt out.

"Well, as I said you've waited all this time for me and it's like you're the one that's meant for me because it's sort of like, I don't know, that means that you'll always be there for me and I need someone like that."

"Oh." My heart was filled with anxiety; it was tearing me apart.

"You do still love me ... right?"

"I ... ah ..." I did ... of course I did, but the words were not coming naturally. What was wrong with me? "Yes, I still love you."

"Good!" She smiled and waved to me as she walked away.

The next few days were good. We said hello to each other and we smiled and waved every day. Her friends would talk to me about her and I would respond with shy statements about my feelings. I was shy, but I was also extremely happy. I felt that my life would come together now. All of that waiting was worth something. There was no amount of badness that could bring me down, I was the most powerful person in the world! I screamed out in joy at every opportunity.

Sometimes I would just sit and watch her. She was so beautiful. Every feature that she possessed was completely perfect. She was the perfect human being to me. I wanted to kiss every single inch of her little face. Every night for the last two years I had imagined myself holding her. She had become my obsession. The Blair in my mind, I knew far better than the real her, I realised. But now there was a chance.

Christmas was coming soon. I planned a BIG present for her. I was so excited. I kept it a secret from everyone. Well ... everyone except for Aria. Aria was one of Blair's friends. She was nice and sweet, from what I could tell, and so I trusted her opinions and secrecy in relation to my Christmas present for Blair.

Blair and I sent messages to each other now. The most exciting part of them being the fact that she sent me love hearts. I sent them to her, as well. I couldn't believe that she was thinking this way towards me ... I had always dreamt it would happen but chose to instead try to make her as happy as possible.

This was challenging because for a long time I put her happiness before my own. This didn't benefit anyone. All it did was cause me pain. But none of that mattered now because Blair loved me! Blair loved me! Blair loved me! Blair loved me! The ACTUAL Blair. The most beautiful and amazing and perfect girl in the world loved me! I could feel everything heading towards a happy future. Blair and I travelling the world together and sharing our love for each other. That's all I needed in life. All I needed was her. She was my world. In my mind she was everything. Absolutely everything.

We got married at the age of twenty and moved to

Spain where we had three children named Mick, Ben and Laura. The end.

I HOPE YOU ENJOYED THE story of how my wife and I came to be together. Now I would like to share with you our story together over the following fifteen years of our happy marriage. Enjoy.

Isn't my sense of humour enormous? That didn't happen. The love hearts stopped being sent. She told me that it all had to slow down. I asked why. It was several days before she told me. Her emotions were scrambled and she didn't know who she loved. As far as I was concerned, if you didn't know who you loved you weren't truly in love. We fell away from each other. I wanted her to stay, but she left. I wanted her to stay. But she left. I wanted her to stay … but she left …

She would come back. She would. We were meant to be together.

She was mine now. She was.

She wasn't.

The animal fell to the ground, dead. A smile rose on the figure's face.

Ashlee was a girl that went to my school. She was in the same grade as me. She didn't like Blair very much. At some point I must have entered a conversation with her because I remember her telling me that Blair was a heartless bitch and that it wasn't surprising that she had done this to me. Ashlee may not have been empathetic, but she was sympathetic, and when Blair found another boyfriend, one with the same name as me, she was there as support. Even with as little as it could do to erase the pain, sometimes, if I was lucky, it lessened it ... if only for a little while.

THE NEXT FEW YEARS PASSED like a rocket. Well, they didn't, but it feels that way now. Ashlee was there for me throughout this entire emotional roller coaster ... but these days we aren't as close. Blair faded from my affections, although it took a very long time. I gained new affections for Aria. But they passed too. And in time I realised I was as stupid and human as everyone else. I could write for days about the feelings I felt through individual parts of this. But now ... now I see that that wouldn't matter. Not in the wake of something else.

Grace. She is my pillow. I think at some point in my emotional journey I gave the name "pillow" to the things that comforted me. She became the biggest of them all. And so I was sitting at my desk. With my memories and the promise of future comfort. But also ... a story. I don't know where it came from but it was sitting on my computer desktop. It goes as follows.

Chapter Two

"**R**AYDIUM! GET DOWN HERE!**" **RAYDIUM** passed, instinctually, through his doorway (which had no door), down the stairs that, in all practicality, served no real purpose but to send an illusion of a second story, and into the small room his family called the kitchen.

His mother was chopping some bizarre life form that was claimed to be a vegetable, but looked more like a mutated rat that had been dyed purple.

"Yes, Mother." Raydium waited.

His mother finished her chopping and placed the vegetable inside a pot filled with water. "See if you can't get this boiled for us, dear."

"What's the point? It's just a waste of time," he replied.

His mother sighed, pausing for a moment, an expression of sorrow seeping onto her face, as it often did. "It's ... it's nice to have it boiled. It makes it seem ... nice."

"It's not nice, Mum. It's not nice and it never will be."

Raydium grabbed the pot and walked out into the street. They lived in the Western District of the city. It was supposed to be the well-off residential area, but Raydium didn't buy it. Perhaps the average income was higher than the other district, but the Eastern District was where all the money was, albeit in the pockets of a few select individuals.

He looked up to see the tallest building in the city, a place he had never even been near. He had heard they were going to knock it down and build something else. Raydium was determined to get rich and live in a building such as that. That's what his father would have wanted him to do – get rich and help Mum.

In general, the Western District got less supplies. Probably for a combination of two reasons: health supplies were made in the Eastern District, and that's where the majority of the population lived.

Raydium thought it was odd that the pattern of the city's welfare went as follows: extremely wealthy, extremely poor and THEN somewhat sustainable. He was suspicious about what was really going on in the government.

RAYDIUM ARRIVED AT THE SMALL building where everyone in the Western District got their electricity. There were crowds of people at this time of the day, all waiting in long lines. Or simply 'splatters' to cook their various dinners. Raydium always stood in line, even though the splatters got you in faster. This was because he knew that generosity got you respect. He would even let those with more of a load go in front of him. He quickly made friends, and he knew that this was the way to even have a chance of making any money, or getting a job.

Raydium's mother worked at the plantation, where the district's food was grown. But maintaining the food products wasn't the most well-paid job.

Raydium wanted to become a head worker. As a head worker he would be paid slightly better, and have the opportunity to be raised to one of the guards, and eventually gain power among the companies. It wasn't easy, though. Head workers were only put into power when a previous one died or was unable to do his job.

There was the head worker of food processing – he essentially ensured that no one was taking more than their fair share, regulating people's intake. Money was symbolic of someone's status; it couldn't actually be used to improve one's living conditions (unless you had enough to buy yourself out). An area's wealth was stagnant and maintained: an economy based around various levels of poverty.

There were the managers of infrastructure, and managers for practically anything else that people could take advantage of. No one was allowed to become too well off. For things like the electricity, there were always guards watching to ensure no one took too long, to keep everyone moving.

When it finally came to be Raydium's turn, he lifted the pot up onto the stove, and pressed the red button. In a few minutes, the contents were boiled. The city DID have advanced technology but most of it was hoarded. It was impossible to know how much more was kept hidden away. Raydium always imagined the technology the richest of the city must have. But for him, advanced stovetop technology was the height of it. And it wasn't even his.

As he maneuvered his way back out of the crowd, an encounter erupted between two men who had obviously been arguing. The crowds dispersed around them as they began to take their conflict into the realm of physicality. The guards moved in to deal with them. The first of the guards aimed towards the closest man and fired his armament. It lashed out at the man, tearing his right leg off. The second man's posture changed to that of prey. A second guard fired towards him, but Raydium never saw the result, as he was pushed into the fray by a fearful woman. The guard, seeing it only as an act of aggression, lowered his weapon with great force into Raydium's skull, and he fell to the ground, unconscious.

R AYDIUM WOKE UP SEVERAL HOURS later in an alien location. In his thoughts, he reasoned that he must be at home, under the care of his mother, as any child would expect. Except he wasn't quite at home, and this wasn't quite a world of comfort and care.

He sat up and found himself lying somewhere next to a glowing light. He reasoned again, getting closer this time to the truth: it must have been nighttime. Nighttime may mean sleep for some, but for a citizen of this city it meant danger. The addicts grew more violent during the night; the reason for this was unknown, but what WAS known was that during the night, if one valued their life, they were to stay inside, lock the doors and bar the windows. It was evident to Raydium that he was outside.

"Have some, kid," a voice spoke from the gloom.

"Ah ... I don't ..." Raydium tried to stand.

"You don't? Well, we all do at some point."

Raydium felt something being pressed up against his mouth; he tried to resist, but before he could prevent it, it was inside. It numbed his senses, and opened them up to a more spiritual world, where there was no such thing as resistance. It was rapidly absorbed into Raydium's system. In that moment there was a change.

He didn't see the world anymore. He felt it. The moon was a ball of light, a huge thought, hanging over the world: a single mind. He heard the voices of billions of organic brains, most of them dull, but some shone through the web of spirituality.

Raydium's mind was drawn to these, he entered them, he was filled by them, and then he travelled on through a world that had no comprehension of space or time. Everything was simply a single point. Movement was an idea – an amusement, unnecessary, but wonderful like a waterfall of laughter that promised its victims that it would never end.

Raydium could conceptualise the point that was the city. But beyond ... calling out like a lamp in the darkness was a point filled with thoughts that would once have seemed alien but now felt like a long-lost friend. Raydium entered into them. There was an allusion of companionship, but soon, this devolved into a burning sensation, as Raydium's flight began to collapse.

"YOU ARE NOT PURE." A billion united voices spoke. "YOU HAVE ABUSED OUR LIFE FORCE. BE GONE. BE GONE."

Like the snap of a stick, Raydium was back. Left in

him was an inner anger and resentment. Held back only by an overwhelming regret. He looked up to examine his surroundings; the man that had forced this upon him was now standing in the flame Raydium had woken to, burning and screaming. Raydium jumped up and ran. With each step what he had just experienced fell further and further from his mind.

RAYDIUM REFUSED TO LEAVE HIS room for what was days but felt, to him, like years. His friend, Fern, came to his door each day and tried to convince him to come out.

"Come on, Ray! What's wrong with you?"

But Raydium never stirred. He feared sleep for it brought back the voices to his mind. Why were they angry at him? Why did they hate him? There was a growing feeling that he meant less and less to the world as time went on.

Mixed with this was a realisation that the world itself meant nothing, as well. Thus, his emotions of isolation and fear at hatred directed at him and emotions of anger and frustration at the shortcomings of that which was around him burned as a conjoined fire within his mind. One voice was increasingly powerful ...

"TAKE THEM. TAKE THEM. DESTROY THEM."

It was in this the primary reason he would not leave his room was revealed. Yes, he felt a pain for the world; it was sick and he could no longer bear it ... but he could not shake the desire to grab Fern by the head and destroy him ... and so it went on, for far too long a time for anyone to know for sure.

Clocks, watches and other such devices were unheard of to most of the city's population. Some tried to mark the days, but this was always forgotten for something deemed more important. When surviving each day is a challenge, one tends to forget other things. Things that the rich take for granted: entertainment and schedules. Raydium recalled his mother talking to him, when he must have been much younger.

"No, no, no, Raydium! Don't go near them, dear. Those people aren't safe."

He recalled how his father had responded. He had taken him aside when his mother collected food from a stall.

"Do you believe they are 'unsafe', Raydium?"

Raydium, young as he was, thought deeply about what his father was trying to ask.

"They ... hmm ... they just look like people to me, Daddy." Raydium looked up into his father's eyes, fearing that he was wrong in saying this, as his mother would surely believe.

"That is true, my son. We are all human beings. Together, in this life. It is easy for some to forget that. Especially when some of us do something that is wrong."

Raydium thought deeply once again. He was confused that two people that were both very important to him could have such differing opinions.

"Why do people do the wrong thing ...?"

His father took his son by the hands. "I'm not going to lie to you, son. It is in our nature. It always has been and it always will be. But it ISN'T all there is. There is love. There is always love: companionship and empathy. Never forget that. Never allow the evils of the world to darken your heart."

"I won't ... Daddy."

Only one thing would raise Raydium from his depressive sickness. Raydium's mother, a forty-year-old woman with a cold determination went, due to the absence of her son's assistance, to boil her food matter herself. It would be a preferable truth to be said that Raydium, embarrassed of making his mother do this herself, left his bedroom and, sprinting down the street, took the pot from her and did his job himself.

In this city, a woman is not safe wandering the streets. But Raydium did not leave his room due to responsibility, he left it due to grief.

Her body was found by Fern's father; he screamed out at the men that surrounded her, and they scattered, unwilling to fight an angry man wielding a frying pan. Fern's father, John Reo, fell to the ground, his stomach lining splattering the stone beneath him. That is where he would stay for several minutes, his senses numbed and instantly traumatised by the condition of the woman he had called his friend. John had made a promise.

"Look after them, John."

"No. No. Michael! Michael!"

His best friend's wife now lay, dead, just as he had himself, and once again, John had failed to save someone dear to him.

Raydium spent the next few days living in Fern's house, where he spoke little and ate less. His and Fern's friendship was old. Raydium's father, Michael, and Fern's father, John, had been friends throughout most of their lives, and the companionship had been adopted in the next generation. However, the majority of the time Raydium and Fern had spent together was in their younger years, when children are still developing and have a ripe taste for adventure and exploration. Those days seemed to pass when Raydium's father died.

The two families maintained pleasantries but a vital link had been severed. Fern's mother had disappeared years ago, leaving John to raise him alone, thus Fern never had much of a mother figure, and, to Raydium's disgust, would often allude that Raydium's mother would become his as well.

Brynn Goal, her name was, after adopting Michael Goal's name. Marriage was dealt with in one of two ways in the city: through ceremony or through documentation. It really depended on status. Generally speaking, there were a few wealthy families in either district that weren't wealthy enough to inhabit the giant skyscrapers, but neither were they poor enough to live a common lifestyle. They lived in mansions that were heavily fenced off and had great expanses of land, containing shopping centres, luxury restaurants and anything they desired. It was these groups, and surely the richer population, that would participate in ceremonious marriage. Firework displays, aeroplanes exploding, essentially anything that showed off wealth and made a loud noise appeared at a wedding. There was no need to write on an official piece of paper saying 'so and so are married' because everyone already knew. What made it all the more exclusive was that the taboo of marrying one's relatives had been overlooked years ago.

Rare was the bride or groom that crossed the classes. Often marriage was used to obtain more power, a family would pay to marry into a wealthier family, and so it went on. However, for the poorer of society, one would have to pay to have documents made saying that two people were married. They both had to be from the same district and sub-district and one (generally the male, depending on their wealth) was required to surrender all of their wealth, so that a married couple essentially had the assets of a single person.

Such was the way of Brynn and Michael Goal's marriage. No ceremony, and hardly a significant celebration. In fact, they both worked that day, and only saw each other in the early hours of the morning and the fringes of late evening. For all the lack of beauty there is to such an event, funeral traditions for the rich happened to be all the more lavish, and for the poor, devastating.

Deaths were so common that incinerators were stationed throughout the city. Raydium did not sit at the base of a gravestone to bid his mother farewell; he was to watch as her body was flung without care into the jaws of a flaming monstrosity.

He ran to stop the guards but they merely electrocuted him without a second thought, not enough to kill him but enough to paralyse him.

Raydium lay on the ground, unable to move, listening to the sound of his mother burning, and for the second time in his life he was watching on helplessly as someone that meant the world to him was stolen from his already brutal life.

He recalled, certainly not for the first time and likely

not for the last, watching his father leave for work, walking down the street as he always did. In a few seconds he would turn around and wave to Raydium, gesturing with his thumb as Raydium had come to rely on. Except he never did.

Raydium would never know exactly why, perhaps the man was on drugs, perhaps he was just angry and his father had been in the wrong place at the wrong time. But nevertheless it happened. It must have been homemade. It certainly wasn't sophisticated like the devices the guards carried. But all the same the sharp object pierced Michael Goal's heart. Had he been a target? Perhaps not. After all, the man had gone on to kill three other men before the guards were on his tail. He was never caught, the man.

Raydium had watched, not fully understanding what he had seen, and as John Reo fell to the ground at his father's side and spoke the last words he would hear, his father was taken away for dead. No investigation, nothing, just termination of a corpse that wasn't even fully dead yet. But it was in these darkest of moments that Michael Goal showed that despite everything he still had just one priority, above even that of his life.

As Raydium looked on at his father's weakening body being carried away, his hand fell limp, perhaps a sign of death, but Raydium could tell otherwise, for seconds before being rounded around a corner, Michael Goal's hand gestured a thumbs-up, as a final farewell to his only son.

He was taken by a truck; they knew he had no family now, and it was the perfect opportunity to harvest him. Still paralysed, Fern and his father fought valiantly to stop them. Fern simply grabbed hold of Raydium, but it was his father's grasp on the boy's leg that was saving him. But against several guards there was an inevitability for defeat.

John Reo was delivered a fatal blast, his last words the final ally Raydium would have in the city as Fern was pulled from him, his ultimate fate uncertain, and Raydium was locked into the vehicle.

Darkness and silence followed, marred only by the sounds of the truck moving. Raydium wondered if he was the only one in the truck compartment. It was so dark that there could have been any number of people in there with him. If there was, though, he doubted he would gain anything from speaking to them. So instead of making any sound himself, he sat, and allowed one of many tears that had made his body their home fall. Many others followed, and eventually he discarded his hesitation in allowing them to.

He was thrown into a crowd of other children, all being herded towards something he couldn't even begin to guess at. There was a man standing, watching over them; as he gained in proximity, he heard the conversation between him and the guard.

"Sir ... Mr Clayton, sir, there's an important message for you."

Mr Clayton's eyes did not stir from the gaze he held fixed on the children. He stood with a large projectile weapon in his hand and would likely fire upon any children that moved outside of the railings.

"What is it," he replied to the guard without extending his speech to a question.

"Sir, the ..."

Raydium did not catch the remainder of the conversation as a commotion was building at what must have been the front of the line. The guards that stood outside of the rails moved forward in an anticipating fashion.

The two girls that stood next to Raydium began crying loudly. The older of the two squinted her face and held back her gasps, pulling the younger girl in her arms and whispering what must have been words of comfort. One boy that stopped walking was belted by a nearby guard. He screamed out.

"Hey!"

The guard that had made it his job to deal with the boy looked up at Mr Clayton, who nodded. The guard called over to another guard and the two of them grabbed the boy, taking him to the front of the line, where Raydium could not see.

The noise that had been coming from the front grew louder, and Raydium and the two girls watched on in shock as the boy who had just been taken to the front ran, jumping over the railing and across the chamber.

Mr Clayton cooly fired a projectile at the boy; it expanded into a net and covered the boy's entire body, electrocuting him whenever he moved. The younger of the two girls at Raydium's side, petrified with fear, used this opportunity to duck underneath the railing on the opposite side. Her elder screamed, chasing after and yelling.

"Sarah! Sarah! NO!"

But it was too late. The guards on both sides leapt after

the girls, firing shots into the air. Every child still in the line fell to the floor, fearing for their lives and screaming.

Raydium was bent down next to a boy that must have been far older than anyone else there. In his hands he held a young child that couldn't have been older than two.

The guards were still firing into the air, and Raydium could hear the two girls being throttled, their screams blocked by the hands of men. Raydium was shivering with fear; sweat poured from his face. He was panting. The boy in front of him holding the child looked into his eyes.

"You ever had to look after someone?" the boy said.

"Ah ... n...no." Raydium replied, confused. The boy handed him the two year old; Raydium wasn't too much younger than the boy so the weight wasn't an issue, yet he looked to the boy with a question on his face. The boy pointed to an archway in the corner of the chamber.

"That looks like the only safe way out."

Raydium opened his mouth to reply but never got the chance. Raydium was afraid, but Ben's expression was ten times worse, and yet he smiled.

"I'm Ben Sheen. Sheen. Get him home."

Raydium watched as Ben stood up, and with all of his strength cried, "ARARRRRRRRRRRRRRRRR!" as he jumped across the railing, grabbing it and throwing it at the guards who were still struggling with the two girls.

Mr Clayton was furious, unleashing his weapons full ferocity. Everyone was still on the ground, except for Raydium. He stood, and, still holding the young child, ran for the archway at the side of the chamber, scared out of his mind, but not willing to look backwards save it be the difference between life and death.

As Raydium made it through the archway and up the stairs it led to, he heard the sound of a large metal object against flesh, and one final scream as a gunshot sounded. There was silence. He heard Mr Clayton order the children to continue moving and Raydium heard the footsteps of over a hundred children. He should have wanted to help them, but he really didn't. Just when he thought he was safe, footsteps began to climb the stairs behind him.

"We know you're up there, kid! Come back to the line!"

Raydium panicked and stumbled further into the room, tripping and landing on an object that fell under his weight. It was a lever. He heard the sound of an engine building in energy and as he looked at its source he saw a great machine with many lights flickering and buzzing for a dozen unknown reasons.

He could feel a guard's presence in the room. "What the ..."

Before the guard or Raydium could do anything, the machine had released a beam of energy that hit Raydium right in the head. He could not see, and gradually, he could not feel anything at all.

Raydium was somewhere different now ... a yellow clam fell onto the ground in front of him.

A Decade Later

H E SAT AT HIS GREAT oak desk and frowned down at the beings that approached him. The largest of them held a small pad of papers and shivered violently on the spot. There was silence in the room as he waited, not wasting his time in being the first to speak.

"Sir?" The smallest of them spoke, but he still did not stir from his icy position.

"Master?" The largest of them stepped forward, his long brown nose dripping with sweat. Yet still, he did not react to the words they spoke.

"We've brought the reports, sir, master." The third creature that stood at a safe distance from his desk piped up in a voice lacking confidence.

The man behind the desk reached out his arm for the papers, his fingers agile and long while containing an unknown, unimaginable power. Startled, the creatures took a cumbersome step backwards. The one holding the pad of papers fell, dropping them on the red tinted carpet. The man did not appear angered, he simply lowered his hand with a silent menace.

"I'm so sorry, sir, it won't happen again, I swear! It was an accident!" the creature gasped as it tried to get back to its feet. But the fear inside it was far too great; it would never know what was coming next.

The other two watched on in horror, for the man, with a flick of his wrist, sent the creature plummeting through the floor, where it would meet instant death. The two remaining creatures stumbled helplessly to pick up the papers. They hurriedly placed them on the man's desk and, now fearing for their lives, ran for the doorway.

The man closed it with a single thought. "It seems you do not realise that we still have business."

"You're going to make us rich!" the fat man chuckled.

"We shall ALL be rich, my dear collaborator, and with the power that comes with it we shall change everything."

The man strutted around the chamber the two men were standing in, his pride evident, although an ancient strain still made its mark on his face.

"I'll never understand how people can be so stupid as to believe that more of this ... stuff ... will help them!" The man sat down, a bun in his hand, alcohol running down his cheeks.

The man stopped his walking, pausing for a moment. "It is all they have."

"But it cannot give them wealth."

"Perhaps, in time, WE will."

The chamber fell silent. The man had tapped at something untouched by discussion for centuries. If he was not careful, it would be perceived as a challenge.

"... They are not like us."

The fat man placed down his bun. "That is why we are here, and THEY are down there."

The man did not respond, instead wandering over to the window, where he examined the view he had observed the world from many times. The tallest building in the whole city, simply known as the Bark Building. "Have YOU ever had Bark?"

The fat man ceased eating, a rare event. "Once ... just

once. How much Bark can it make? Can it feed them all?"

The man, still staring out the great windows of his highest chamber, took in once more the long, winding streets of Bark City that stretched as far as the eye could see.

"Yes."

He sat at his great oak desk and frowned down at the report. Things had gotten worse. Thirty-four percent of civilians in Bark City now supported the revolution. It wouldn't be long before it could be enacted; wealth would mean nothing.

A woman had been attacked along the Western Wall for carrying Bark. This would not happen in any other part of the city. People were beginning to realise the effect of Bark on their lives.

A creature entered the room. "Sir. I was told you should see this, sir." The creature placed a projector on the man's desk and left the room.

He played the footage. Images of Bark City were accompanied by musical tunes, which soon faded.

A face appeared; it spoke aggressively: "We have all been misguided into believing Bark is a safe recreational drug. We have all been misguided into believing Bark is a safe recreational drug! It affects our lives. It forces us to want it. Without our knowing it has squirmed into our society and taken away those things we used to treasure so highly. Do you remember, people of Bark City? Do you remember Rimbledale?"

The footage ended. The man sat back in his chair, his hand covering his mouth, a way to hold back his anger. They didn't understand. The revolution was going to ruin everything. This was his only chance to put things right, and the fools were going to ruin it all!

His hard work and persistence were being delivered back to him in tatters. He had known something had to be done. But it seemed he would need to go one step further. He would need to make an example of them.

The creature that had brought the projector returned to take it back. The man stood, grabbed the creature by the neck, and broke it.

H E TURNED THE FINAL CYLINDER and the vault opened. He stepped inside the room that contained 66% of the money in the whole of Bark City. Gold was everywhere; the walls were made of it. Diamonds crusted even the dullest parts of the vault. Tables built from fine materials sat in the corners, where they were set as if for the most extravagant meals, yet none ever sat at them. Large gems adorned everything, and these were polished at least five times each day. Piles of coins, stacks of ingots, wealth beyond imagining were all contained in this vault, going on and on further than one could see, and all of it served no purpose but power.

There was enough wealth in this one chamber to feed ten cities the size of Bark City, and yet it wasn't even used to feed ONE ... it was used to control it. On the wall furthest from him hung a portrait of his late wife, Iopathalla Tramsuldine. She had been killed by members of the revolution, back when they only existed outside of the city.

He recalled that night in impeccable detail, from the most intimate moments, to the most traumatic. It had been many years ago, in a better time, when he had seen things differently, when there was hope. He rummaged through the treasures of the vault until he reached what he had been searching for. There existed only two of these ancient artifacts in the world, and for good reason. It possessed the power to transform 12 selected portions of matter into any material known to the user. This one had already been used 10 times, but he intended to use the next transformation in a way that would have an effect for a great length of time. Because THEY didn't know of its limitations.

When he walked the streets, people stared. Because he was the only one wearing clothes. The streets were filled with the poor, hungry and homeless. They had no one to beg to because everyone was begging.

The alleys were horrific: dead bodies littered the paths, being eaten by animals ... or starving people. Brawls broke out incessantly over who would get to eat the next dead child. Life in its purest form: uncensored survival. And then there were the Bark trucks. Tagged with the logo 'Barkose', the company responsible for the distribution of Bark as well as being one of the central organisations of government over Bark City.

When these trucks arrived, even those fortunate enough to live in a house unlocked their extensive (though unsophisticated) security systems and ran forth into the streets; Bark was everything. The fighting stopped, the eating stopped. Bark. The man walked onward, into the richer district of Bark City, the Western District. The richer district, but also the district with the most 'new ideas'.

It was here that the man would find the culprit behind the footage that had been broadcast to all those living in Bark City who were able to receive it: 44%. Swarms of starving children tried to leap at the man, an obvious source of resources. Men and women forgot their previous activities as they ran towards him, begging to him or trying to fight him. But all of them were met by a nod of the man's head, followed by a broken bone, a muscle tear, the absence of an organ, or death.

The man arrived at his destination. The rebels made their way out to meet him, knowing his face.

"Traitor," said the man who made himself the obvious leader. He was the same man who spoke the words that he had come to extinguish. "We trusted you. You promised you'd help us. But yet we remain here, surviving on food unworthy for even the most horrid individuals while you sit up in your precious Bark Building eating food that should be for everyone!"

With that several men ran with weapons in hand towards the man. But before they reached him, they were slaughtering themselves with their own armaments.

"I will keep my promise." The man raised the device, and the leader of the revolution became Bark.

There were noises coming from the bottom floor. For a time, he ignored them. But a few minutes proved the noises all the more incessant. Yet he still stopped to consider his success. The message had been made clear: they were simply resources to him and escaping his power was impossible. No doubt, the addicts among them would feel compelled to feast on their leader. A demoralising event, indeed.

Mr Clayton, the manager of Barkose, entered the man's office and announced greetings solidly. "Hello, Mr

Clayton. What brings you here on this fine evening?"

Mr Clayton stood rigidly, examining the man's demeanour. "The children ... they are ready."

"Ah, yes. Well. I already have a full stock. There may not be any need, sir."

Clayton's expression darkened further. "Make a need."

The man stiffened in slight fear. "It isn't right, sir. We don't need to—"

"The army will need to be large ... my dear friend..." Clayton cut in.

"You don't mean?"

"I do. I wish to see the machine. Now. And a demonstration, if you please."

The man held back an expression of reservation and stared at the floor for as long as he could get away with. The thoughts of times long ago flowed through his mind, until he was close to being dissolved into them. A voice inside him screamed out into the void that had become his Soul. Yet it was still there; he felt it there each time he used it. But how could it have become so corrupt? We all have our own passage of learning, they had told him. It never did matter, but money did ... still.

He led Clayton down to the bottom floor. The man clicked his fingers and several of the brown creatures ran off into the corners of the room. Before them stood a large vessel, with conveyors on either side.

"Impressive. Now make it work."

The man's fingers clicked once more, and the brown creatures reappeared, two children bound between them. A girl and a boy. Clayton watched with a smirk as the girl was thrust into the vessel. It lit up into billions of individual shades of light and made great sounds like the crack of a baseball bat on concrete.

The boy screamed, "Why? WHY? Let us go!"

The brown creatures grabbed him, but they could not hold him down. Sparks shot from his hands, wildly flinging themselves across the room in no conceivable pattern. He had power, but not control. The man raised his hand, and sparks emitted from his hands, as well; however, they backfired on him in the microseconds before they made contact with the boy – why, the man would not know until after the encounter.

The man was sent flying back across the room. The boy turned red with anger, and with a nod of his head, sent a delta wave straight for the man's head.

However, the man was far more experienced, and reacted accordingly, his delta wave neutralising the boy's.

The boy ran.

Clayton tried to stop him, but was throttled by a lash from the boy's eyes. He was gone. The man reached to assist Clayton. They both stood and watched, flustered, as the little girl came out of the vessel on the opposite side. Although, she was no longer a little girl. In her place stood a small, repulsive, brown creature.

"Master."

Four bodies were being lifted into a truck to be removed from the house they had been found in. Three of them were dead. One was alive. The three dead had been slaughtered by the fourth. Mrs. Clayton stamped the names onto the official papers:

Fern Reo

John Reo

Brynn Goal

She looked down at the child that had been collected. "So ... you did this?"

"Where's the man? ... WHERE'S THE MAN? IN THE BARK BUILDING?"

"Bark Building? What are you going on about? You mean the big old thing up there? It's been empty for years. You really do have something wrong going on in that head of yours ... don't you?" She chuckled.

The child was lifted onto the truck violently.

Mrs. Clayton stamped the final name:

Raydium Goal

There were also some notes attached to the story when I came across it:

Authority/Hierarchies

Poverty

Ambition

Drugs

Love/Hate; Positive and Negatives

Rebellion

---> ray becomes man

---> ray that is a boy when the man is 25

Depression

The Rimbledale Trees produce Bark, they sing, and their vocalisation takes on a solidified form; Bark. However, when the Bark is consumed, it liquifies, and an essential value of the tree's life is subtracted.

The Bark Building houses Tree slaves that are harvested, but over time the Bark's effects will weaken.

Because of this, Barkose is building an army from the impoverished citizens of the Eastern District's children, to invade Rimbledale and take more trees.

Bark is most prominent during the day. Corrupted Bark sources weaken at night, and thus cause individuals with a Bark addiction to feel emotions of psychotic regret and anger.

But the thing that frightened me was the text right at the bottom:

Chasing Pillows

Chapter One: Who Am I?
Chapter Two: What Am I?
Chapter Three: Why Am I?
Chapter Four: The Voices
Chapter Five: The Conflict
Chapter Six: The Madness
Chapter Seven: The Pillows

Notes: Questioning of self, inner worlds, cases where the question doesn't exist.

A layout of ... me? My life? Why was there a description of my life story and ... possibilities? As if I was a character of fiction? And if it was about me ... then what separated me from the story of Raydium Goal? Neither stories were complete.

Chapter Three

This next chapter contains a few things that Opaulde wrote over the course of a year. He did not write much for a while. But these are the things I have managed to compile.

—*Darcy*

HELP ME!

Give me a moment to stop splattering my nervousness hormones all over the floor.

Okay. All right. Yep. So.

Let me tell you this in a story? Okay?

Prepare for the worst date idea ever ... In fact, don't read on if you value your mind ...

On the 29th, tomorrow, Chris and I are going to get together to discuss the following and to scout out the place for possibilities and specific details that she will never have to know about anyway. So on the 30th when I may be doing your thing, I get to see her, right?

Well, I'm going to tell her that she has the option to come with me on an adventure on the 15th of next month. If she says yes my rough estimation is that I'll tell her to meet me in the Square at 10 a.m. If that's not a complete disaster there will be a document 'waiting there for us'.

Now you know she loves Doctor Who. The document is signed: 'To Opaulde and Grace from The Doctor'. It is a map. It shows our current location and a pathway to two Xs on it as well as some other symbols denoting locations and the like.

First, it leads to the Elizabeth Mall. There I intend to buy the two of us something to mark the occasion. The map then leads out of town and to an X that represents a package. The package contains two Doctor Who books and another message from The Doctor. It is a riddle that tells us that the other X is essentially on the way to the Gardens. We go.

The second package is a small TARDIS. Inside it is another message from The Doctor that simply states: 'Have a picnic. Picnics are cool.' And so I take her to the part of the Gardens that has the large clock. I unpack the picnic stuff. We eat. At this point I have some things to say. I tell her that she has to listen very carefully. She is to listen to the questions I have to ask but is not to answer them using words. I will offer her something and if she accepts this something that will be her way of saying yes. If she does not that is a no.

I ask, "Grace. Will you be my girlfriend? And. Would

you like a jelly baby?" 'Would you like a jelly baby?' is a reference from Doctor Who.

Even if this is terrible ... don't tell her anyway. Don't say anything.

Please.

Please.

I'm very emotional about it ...

IN AUSTRALIA, A WIDELY ACCEPTED opinion is that asylum seekers are 'illegal immigrants', and that they have no right to travel to Australia by boat. They are branded as Boat People, invaders from other countries, and are even excluded from any association of being human. By definition, asylum seekers are not illegal immigrants, and thus anyone who travels to Australia as a legitimate asylum seeker has the right to seek safety. It is, of course, possible that these asylum seekers are actually illegal immigrants; however, the sincerity of their claims should always be checked extensively, and if they are found to be true asylum seekers, they should be processed and sent somewhere where they can find asylum. This is a legal process that is acceptable by law.

Australia's population is roughly 22 million, which, on a global scale, is a very small amount indeed. When you consider that many major countries around the world have cities with the equivalent population, it opens your eyes to the relatively small amount of people in our country. Therefore, any claims that asylum seekers are overfilling our country are greedy and ignorant to the truth, which is that Australia is actually quite unpopulated.

Furthermore, Australia is responsible for thousands

of asylum seekers each year, while other countries, such as Greece, expect millions more asylum seekers every year. This also highlights Australia's ignorance and greed towards the situation. An example of this greed is the opinion that Australia should not have to pay tax for the processing of asylum seekers, which is greedy because it is a statement of irresponsibility; it is to say that we should not have to work towards ending these issues.

So what are the conditions that these asylum seekers are coming from? Well, many flee from violence and danger to their lives. They fear that they are endangered, and this leads them to make the decision to seek refuge. As a refugee in some countries, people wait years in poor conditions just to have the opportunity to travel to another country such as Australia.

In conclusion, it is plain to see that asylum seekers have every right to flee their countries to seek safety. Australians are ignorant to these facts; therefore, they believe that they have no right to come to Australia. The general population is ignorant and greedy, and sometimes racist, as they never stop to consider that these people are truly in need.

THE FIRST EVER COMPELLING HYPOTHESIS SUPPORTING THEISM

THE EXISTENCE OF A THEISTIC presence is widely unreasonable.

Believers in a theistic presence are widely unreasonable.

Therefore they are composed of a lack of reason.

Therefore they are the product of the unreasonable.

As a theistic presence represents the unreasonable, believers of a theistic presence are the product of a theistic presence.

Thus a theistic presence exists.

The figure walks over to the animal and begins to skin it.

Dear Reader,

Do you feel my words? Or simply read them?

That, I think, is up to you.

I would very much like to share a thought with you. One I have had in recent days. It is not subject to the judgments of preparation; it is pure. For what is language but emotion given form. Simple, bare, yet sometimes intricate subjectivity.

But that is not what I wish to discuss. Is there (or have I been the victim of a flawless illusion) an aspect within you that deals with your fears, doubts, hopes and aspirations? If this is so, the true purpose of this sharing of thoughts will not be revealed unless you allow your mind to drift to that place. The place where your inner voices chant in both remarkable joy and haunting despair. I do not know you.

What are your doubts? Do you doubt yourself? Perhaps ... others? Or the Universe as a whole?

The former questions often, in this life, lead to the last. I sometimes doubt the Universe. There's a possibility that you do, too. At every turn of the pages of experience there lies uncountable examples of devastation, ignorance, pain and seemingly incurable deficits of society. Is it a better option ... just ending it?

I do hope that you feel my words to this point. For to simply read them is to deny them their dream. Do you recall ... that dream you had denied? The barriers that prevented this dream may have seen you as little more than you may see my words. But if you do feel them:

Is it wrong to simplify all aspects of the Universe as either good or bad? What of the neutral, the impartial, these so-called shades of grey? It is a shame that we do not have the option to discuss these things further, is it not? But I am sure we can agree, there is sadness and happiness in this world: those things that hurt us and those things that heal us.

Even those who find fulfillment in careers, relationships and finance can carry the burden of knowing that there are things that are wrong in the Universe. But I offer: without this sadness, without discontent, who would be there to stand up and say that something is wrong? Without tragic empathy, and pain, who would plead to their fellow men and women to try to change? To work together for a better world? Without sorrow ... who would fight? Eternal happiness is no alternative to a Universe that houses sadness. For it is the nature of our world to evolve.

Reader, I hope that you can see and thus gain hope in knowing that without sorrow, we are not complete. We are trapped. This does not make better the suffering of our societies nor our personal trials. But it CAN give hope. Be glad you can see the flaws around you, for is ignorance to others' suffering really any better?

Thank you,

Love From Stranger

LIFE'S CRESCENDO

No tree stirred

There was no joy, hope, nor glee

Movement was alien to the barren home of reality

No page turned

No word was heard

Drip. Drip. Drip.

The taps sang in low, rapid tones

Frowns fell from fretful faces

Hidden heads heard horrors

"Why is it so?" the clock's tick did ask

But ushered, under untimely umbrellas,

a light did appear, an idea, a thought

a sense of control

A hope

And steps were heard, not as to walk, but as to dance,

songs were sung, smiles were smiled

Like a light bulb in the darkest of rooms,

It was a vista for the short sighted

Curtains were opened

And they did wonder, what lay beyond the horizon

EVIL.

That's what I am.

I see little children abusing things they see as alien.

I see girls gossiping and being cruel.

I see boys being rowdy and foolish.

HATE.

That is what I feel.

A burning rage, insatiable by anything less than death.

But the death of others?

Or the death of myself?

EMBITTERED.

That's what I am. That is what I feel.

When I realise everything that is wrong with the world exists within me as well.

When I realise my hate is more about me than anyone else.

I hate in others what I don't want to accept in myself.

If what I see is evil is me and it is everywhere, what is good?

Right?

Just?

Nothing.

And nothing can sate my pain.

Except for one thing.

Termination.

This is what I am.

This is what I feel.

Even when I can understand.

Even when I can see why things are.

The facts are still ever present.

And make my heart weary.

Perhaps it has always been so.

Chasing Pillows

Have I always simply blocked it out?

Are the joys of a child playing amongst the trees those of a juvenile clawing for some sanity in this horrid world?

The Universe is simply a machine that makes things.

Is it random?

It doesn't matter.

Because it feels that way.

I remember a time that I was strong.

Or perhaps I was weak?

Who knows.

It's all just chaos now.

Chaos.

Absolute order is futile amongst chaos: perceived just or catastrophic.

I did try once.

It only caused me grief.

Now I must simply be.

If I can.

At least in this state.

Help.

Help.

Help.

Help.

Help.

Help.

Help.

Help.

Help.

Help.

It all evaporated ...

My meaning, my everything, was proved false. And so I'm left as just something that has nothing to go for but every motivation to. Yet motivation always seems to wane. What next? I really don't know.

Know that these things that you have read ... though they may seem distinct ... are connected. I hope that my works, if they form at all, will show the way to a further explanation, such as the one I had intended, but was torn by the trials of a bittersweet world.

Chapter Four

This next story that Opaulde wrote is about love, family and loss. I like to think this was a part of Opaulde's thinking through and learning to express and understand emotions.

—Darcy

The Dying Tree

MY NAME IS ANNA. BUT you don't really need to know that. This isn't really a story about me. It's a story about a friend of mine. It was a friend that came out of nowhere and changed my life forever.

I suppose the best place to start is about three years ago, when I had just started my last year of school. I had arrived, and was excited, above all else, to study

Geography and Architecture. They were the true loves of my life for a very long time. Oh, and History, of course, because nothing is better than reading up on a historical setting, exploring the lives that ancient people lived, and the places they existed in. So, to say the least, I was excited, thrilled, and life couldn't have gotten any more thrilling – except it did.

Well, it did AND it didn't. You see, I did not have many friends. I had almost none, in fact. Perhaps Miranda was what you would call a friend, but she was only a study buddy to me, nothing more. It was a Sunday when she had come over to my place, crying her eyes out because of something some boy had said about her face, or something.

"Miranda," I said, probably with less compassion than was due.

"Don't YOU go off at me! You don't know how it feels because all you care about is your study and blah! Blah! Blah!"

Miranda stormed out of my door, and my mother gave me an inquisitive look.

"Sandwich?" my mother had asked.

"Sure," I replied, and continued my journey into Ancient Roman warfare.

I didn't see Miranda at all during that week. It wouldn't be until the following Sunday that I saw her again – in church. I was seated in the front row, listening to the ranting on that I didn't really want to listen to. But, of course, I had to, because that was how my mother was back then. She was far too religious for my liking.

My study of History had taught me that religion never

led to anything good. It made war, pillage, and just general slaughter and rape. It was also a good thing, of course, in many ways. It helped people come together – sometimes. And made people think about caring for one another and developing beliefs and social customs and laws. But as far as I could see, that was a very small part of something that was mostly misleading and damaging.

My mother knew every last rant and speculation of the mass by heart, and, so did Miranda. She came to the same church that we did. I used to enjoy it, her company, and I suppose I did believe in all this ridiculousness for quite a few years – before I decided to grow a brain. A good brain, I mean. As egotistical as that sounds, it's just my frustration at people's behaviour flooding the planet coming through. I'm a bit of a hypocrite.

I love the architecture of churches and cathedrals, and the Vatican is incredible. So without what I hate, there would never have been what I love. One of those ironies of life, I guess. As the mass went on, my attention grew more and more towards Miranda. She wasn't acting normally. Surely this one boy hadn't upset her THAT much? But what would I know about that? Mating rituals and human urges seemed dumb to me. Although, I swore that I saw her crying. I should probably confront her later on. But I wouldn't do it in the church. God wouldn't be pleased with that. Not formal enough for him.

When I was little, I had this bear that I cared for and treasured above pretty much everything else in my life. It was my friend, and when it was with me, I could just let my imagination fly. But the bear isn't with me now, and I probably won't ever see it again.

When Miranda and I met, I was the dumb one,

and she was the smart, intelligent one. I used to listen to everything she said, and try to replicate it in my own work or the way I made myself appear to the world. She even had me wearing makeup at one point – something that I don't do now and never will again. She made me get rid of my bear; apparently it wasn't 'cool' enough for a girl to carry around with her. Miranda insisted on me having a bag instead. But I saw no point in it; I didn't even use it to hold anything.

I listened anyway, and followed her every piece of advice as to what I should do. I dressed like her, tried to speak like her, and I 'liked' the boys that she liked. But about a year after we first met, I also met a teacher named Mr. Spark.

He was THE most incredible man I had ever met. He was a correct balance of everything you could ever want a human being to be. He was smart, humble, confident, joyous, interesting. In fact, there isn't a single positive word he wasn't. He respected me, something that few people have ever done.

My father died when I was six, so I never really knew him, and my mother never respected a single thing that exited my mouth. To her, there was always something I was doing wrong.

But Mr. Spark saw something in me that I don't think I even did. He taught me everything I know about the world today, and we would debate and discuss everything under the sun to the point where neither of us knew what we were talking about, so we just laughed.

Within the most enjoyable six months I have ever experienced, I realised that I had been following Miranda around like a pet, not even stopping to consider what I was doing. She wasn't smart. No, she didn't know anything about anything. Except for boys, boys, and how to be a 'girl' ... she knew plenty about that garbage, and I had been absorbing all of it.

It was just as I had been indoctrinated into Catholicism by my mother. But not now ... now I knew how to live my own life, to live for me, and for my beliefs! Not something that has been set by God and his chaotic evolutionary 'miracle' called life.

I was walking home from school on a Monday afternoon, and I was concerned for two reasons: Miranda wasn't there today, meaning something must really be wrong, and even though I hated the person she was, I still liked to think that I was helping her, in a way. And even if she was using me, I didn't really care. I choose to live my life in helping other people, like Mr Spark helped me. The second reason I was worried was because my mum hadn't arrived home on Sunday night. Usually she would see me at church, go off on her little binges and then arrive home drunk. The thing was that she hadn't, and I had no idea whether or not she had killed herself from an alcohol overdose, or whether she had been kidnapped and taken away by some psychopath.

I arrived home, and still, no sign of Mum. "Shit, Anna," I said out loud to myself. I had an essay on Ancient Greece and an exam to study for; I really didn't need this on top of all that. But I couldn't just ignore it; I had to go check on her. So I walked down, in the middle of the evening, to the shady place my mum would go to every night to exploit her 'abilities' to all the local men. When I arrived there, my mother was nowhere to be seen, but there was a group of men standing around drinking together, and I had caught their attention.

"Aye, boys, look what we got ourselves here! Some good-looking stuff going on there!" one of them said.

The rest of the group looked me up and down, some whistling at me, others half-laughing, and half-choking through their alcohol-filled guts.

"I'm here for my mother," I said.

"Oooh! This girl knows what she wants!" said one of the men at the back of the pack before nearly slipping in his own drink.

"Just tell me where my mother is," I insisted.

"Maybe after we're done with ya, love, we can make a deal." The man at the front of the group stepped towards me, and I was more than a little scared as he touched my waist, and obviously had intentions to touch a lot more.

"Get off me," I yelped as I pushed him away from me.

"Oh don't be difficult, beautiful, we just wanna have some fun, is all."

The man's mates laughed and chanted in the background, telling him to do all sorts of uncouth things to me. I thought of running, and in that moment, I probably should have. It was a need to find my mother that made me stay. I couldn't bear the thought of her being hurt, even after all the times she had hurt me.

I can remember a time when she was the most amazing woman I knew. She was my female icon and role model that I tried to live up to. Then Dad died, and she was never the same again. I had never been baptised, because originally my parents had wanted me to be able to choose my own beliefs. But that was as far as my freedom went.

Mum went crazy; she would do insane things, like just kicking in a wall or not feeding her and me for days. I grew to hate her, and only now am I able to get over it, like I had to get over everything Miranda had done to me. Because keeping grudges would only hurt me in the end, as Mr. Spark said. But that didn't change the fact that my mother forced me into church each Sunday, made me read the Bible, when I wanted to read adventure books, and the hitting.

She'd hit me whenever I said anything that went against her will, and now, almost in unison with the memory of her hitting me, the man smacked me hard on my behind. I yelped, and all the men moved in closer to me. I was angry, I wanted to just hit them all to the ground, and I tried, whacked the ringleader directly in the temple, and he fell to the ground. Then I resorted to throwing the nearby chairs at any of the other men that came near me, but most of them got to me, grabbed me. They pulled me into the centre of the group and moved in on me. It was terrifying.

But then there was a voice. I wasn't quite sure what it said, but it made the men move away from me, and when the alcohol and muck had finally left my eyes, I was holding my mother's hand, running across the street, and heading back home. Home ... home ... sweet ... sweet ... home.

"Are you okay?" my mother asked when we were safely in our own house again.

"No ... No. No! I am NOT okay!" I screamed at her for what must have been hours, and she just stood there

... listening ... not moving in the slightest.

I just kept yelling and cursing at her. She did nothing to stop me: blank expression, she listened and took it all in. I was certain every house for a mile could hear my life story being shouted out across space, my voice ringing through the walls.

When I was done, Mum sat down in the chair where Dad used to sit. I don't think anyone had sat there since he died. Hmm, no, there had been one person. Daddy's doctor, when he had come in to tell me the bad news. Daddy was gone. Mum looked sad, no, not sad, crushed ... shattered ... destroyed, sitting in that old dusty chair. She opened her mouth several times, but nothing came out. Finally, after what felt like eternity, she muttered just a few words that tore right through my soul.

"Miranda. Your friend. Miranda. She's dead."

The next few days were confusing. I didn't know what I was feeling. Regret? But why? She'd done nothing for me, nothing at all. Yet in my mind I felt that maybe something could have been different. I could have been nicer, kinder, maybe even taught her a little of what I had come to learn about life. Maybe Mr. Spark could have helped her too. Teach her how to think for herself. But was it actually joy I felt? Happiness that someone that had nearly sent me into a spiral of foolishness was now gone? Was it a sense of completion that I was feeling? That now that this chapter had come to an end, things could get better? No. I think it was fear. This whole time: was everything that I had convinced myself into believing ... wrong? Was the way Miranda chose to live the right one? Was my mother right? I wondered, as I saw Miranda's coffin in front of me, was this how life was meant to be? Girls are born, boys are born. Girls learn to be girls, boys learn to be boys. Then a girl meets a boy, they have children, and then they both die and go to heaven, with this system repeating endlessly.

Mr. Spark made me want to believe that life was important without all the religious dogmas and nonsensical jabbering. But was that incorrect? Then yet another feeling came to me, as Miranda's coffin was dropped slowly into the dust. What if it all means nothing? That this existence is just a meaningless pattern of life and death. No heaven, and no creator, just life living for no greater purpose than to live.

I learnt that Miranda had died in a car accident, something that I never thought someone I knew would be involved in. Her whole family had died, I think. Apparently a few had been taken to hospital, but had slim chances of recovery.

I didn't study for my exam, and the essay I needed to do was left undone. I failed both, and my teachers looked at me with pity, because they knew that Miranda was dead. But also with confusion, because most of them had thought that I was never particularly close to Miranda anyway. The truth was that there wasn't enough in Miranda's personality to be close to her. Whether she was my friend or not, I wasn't even sure myself.

I wanted to speak to Mr. Spark about all that had happened to me over those few days, but he had left the school a year before, because the school didn't think they needed him. The school didn't say that, of course, but the truth was plain to see. Probably even to them, but they chose to ignore it.

Like a quote I read once in my studies. I can't

remember exactly what it was, but what it basically said was that it is ever present that individuals will find the truth somewhere along in their lives, but it is also almost certain that most of them will pretend that it never happened, and continue on with their lives without ever considering it again.

I am not one of those people. I see something, and suddenly it is everywhere: in the air I breathe, in the books I read, and in the food I eat. The truth talks to me like God talks to my mother, and it's interesting, really, how so many different people think so many different things about something that should be quite simple. But from little things, big things grow, I suppose. Not always for the better.

So, yes, for weeks, I was lost in my thoughts. Only concentrating enough to work if I really needed to. My mind was the only thing that interested me for a long time. History and ancient buildings, design and inventions seemed boring to me.

It was something completely irrelevant that caught my eye, and it didn't happen in a single day. It happened over about two weeks. The first few days, I noticed this boy, he looked kind of strange, but that never really put me off someone. He was sitting alone on a bench just outside of the school. Yeah, a bit like the 'alone-with-no-friends' stereotype.

He looked blank. There was never a time that I saw his face show the slightest amount of emotion. After about a week, I realised something incredible. He looked uncannily similar to Miranda's little brother. I had only met him twice, once at school, and once at Miranda's house.

The reason why I hadn't recognised him was due to his expressionless features. The two times I had seen him, he had been joyous and cheerful. Now he was like a plastic dummy. Like one of the ones you see in shops sometimes. If it was him, he must have survived the car crash. I couldn't imagine having my whole family die; it must have been terrible. And that is probably a major understatement. I tried to imagine losing my father three times. I couldn't.

I couldn't remember if it was right, but I thought his name was Isaac. As the days went on, I tried getting closer to him to see if my suspicions had any weight to them. I eventually got as close as I possibly could without making him aware, but something told me that he wasn't quite aware of anything that was happening around him at the moment.

I took the time to ask one of the teachers about him; they said that they were giving him some time to recover. Apparently he hadn't said a word since the accident, and was spending all of his time drawing. I wondered, with great curiosity, what he was up to, and despite the fact that he was probably too traumatised to care about me, I decided I would investigate Isaac's drawings.

I went home that night, and Mum was already asleep. I had to make myself dinner, but I didn't mind, because I had more important things to think about.

The following morning, I prepared myself for school as if there was a bomb threat in my house. I was extraordinarily excited to see what would happen today. The passionate Anna was back, and the most amusing thing was, I had no idea why. I guess I just enjoyed the thought of getting the opportunity to work something out. Discovering answers – it is the thing that makes me the happiest.

I arrived at school, and immediately ran down to where Isaac had been over the last two weeks. But to my great disappointment, he wasn't even there. I frowned, but got over it, deciding to come back just after school and see if he was back. When I arrived in my History class, the teacher took me aside from the rest of the group and asked me if I wanted to take a few days off, as I had been acting very upset about Miranda's recent passing.

"No, there's no need for that, Miss. I'm dealing quite well, overall, I think, actually ... I just wasn't thinking straight for a while there ..."

"Okay. But just let me know if you need any extensions, Anna." She smiled.

"Thank you, Miss." I smiled back, and then returned to my seat.

The teacher was rather surprised when I worked at my optimal capacity throughout the lesson. I had returned flawlessly to my A+ level, and had no intention of leaving it ever again.

This was where I thrived, in a classroom, with plenty of juicy subjects to dig into, and a mystery to explore in the real world, too. And that's where things started to get really exciting.

After Science class, I returned to the spot where Isaac had been drawing, and this time, he was there. His face was even paler then it had been before. I felt his pain surge through me. I frowned as I walked over to him to investigate, and my heart stopped, stuck halfway in between happy, thriving Anna, and depressed, life-sucks

Anna.

Isaac didn't even acknowledge my existence; I might as well have been standing a kilometre away from him. From this distance, I could really tell that the only thing that was in this boy's world right now was this drawing. But what was it of?

I examined the page, my extensive knowledge exploring dozens of possibilities in an instant. But none of them correlated to what this thing was. It was exquisitely beautiful; the detail and time he was putting into this one drawing was incredible. But I could not work out what it was of. I came back every day, experiencing the same shift of emotions: I would wake up happy as anything, and clear through my study and work like Leonardo da Vinci, and then watch Isaac as he drew his picture, returning home feeling confused and ever more curious.

A week passed by as I continued to watch Isaac and not once did his features change. But I began to understand his drawing more and more. I couldn't tell what it was, but it had a certain structure to it that was very clear. The amount of detail had tripled a hundredfold since the first time I came over to see him, and whatever it was, was truly beautiful. I knew not how one individual could have the mind to create something as brilliant as this. It was surely up there with the world's most famous artworks. Yet no one would ever see it.

How much talent goes unseen in our world? How much do you think we miss while we are busy worrying about our little issues and dramas? That is the true evil of things such as conflict, war and loss: we forget to live and experience what we love. We become absorbed by so much in our lives that we come to believe that the world is nothing but pointless vulgarity. And all these ideas came to me from the influence of a boy one year younger than me, who I hadn't even spoken to. Yet he had already taught me something that I think was controlling me for a long time. Isaac left the bench, and walked over to a car. Inside was an elderly woman; she spoke to Isaac, who didn't even look her in the eye.

"Isaac ... why don't you just stay home, with me? We can talk about all this." The old woman sounded concerned for Isaac. I watched from a few metres away, hidden from the lady's view, but was still able to see what Isaac did in response.

He turned from his drawing to a fresh piece of paper, and drew with speed that I couldn't believe. He drew two pictures of himself, both in incredible detail for something he drew in a matter of minutes. In one picture, he was happy, and sitting at the bench here at school. In the other, he was sad, and sitting in what must have been a house where he was living in. The picture was so clear, it was amazing. I could never draw something with such a clear image.

The old lady spoke again. "But it's your home. Surely you want to be home, Isaac."

Isaac started to draw what he drew before again, but the old woman stopped him.

"Okay. I understand."

The two of them drove off, and I decided now was the time to walk home. I had a lot to think about, but didn't get much of a chance. I didn't see Isaac for two more days because I was held in for extension work at school.

I thought constantly of his drawing, and asked

myself why he would want to be at school. Why was all this so important to him? And why couldn't he speak? Why couldn't he express his feelings? Was the crash THAT traumatic for him? I concluded that I just didn't understand.

When I saw him next, he was on the bench, again, still drawing. Except this time, I could finally see what the picture was. He had made huge progress since the last time I had seen him. The picture was beautiful. The detail had exploded to a level that I simply could not believe. Something so simple was being shown to me in such a complex, amazing way.

The picture that Isaac was drawing was of a tree. But it wasn't just a drawing; it stood on the page, like any tree would. Tall, and strong, I was almost willing to believe it was real. Perhaps it was. I actually wasn't certain, and it made me wonder, what if there WERE worlds full of trees such as this one, just waiting to be explored by a mind willing to believe?

I remembered my bear, and the adventures we had shared together. What had happened to that little girl that used to play all day long? But I knew the answer to my own question.

Isaac sat there, staring down at his own creation, motionless, as if he no longer had a purpose, and that his work was now complete. I watched, awestruck. About fifteen minutes of silence, Isaac placed his drawing at his side, stood up, and walked away, waiting for the old lady to come and pick him up as usual. Why was he leaving his tree? I expected him to come back for it, but he didn't. He took everything with him, but left the tree sitting there on the bench. Why would he leave something so beautiful alone like that? I stood there, and then lay there, looking at the sky and the clouds for what must have been an hour, pondering, with a frown on my face, why Isaac would leave his drawing. In the end, I decided I wouldn't allow it. I grabbed the picture and ran home.

On the way to school in the morning, I looked over Isaac's tree. It had a lot more to say than I had first thought. The tree had lots of animals playing around inside it, and even more around its base. The leaves were lush and looked green despite their colourlessness. It was beautiful in every way possible. It reminded me of my dad.

I was Daddy's baby tree, and he was my big Daddy tree. He had big lush leaves full of knowledge and wisdom, and animals would play around and inside him like the ebbing paths of life.

I almost forgot that I had to do school stuff from spending too much time looking over the tree and smiling to myself. I didn't really concentrate on my school work; I just did what I needed to do to get through it. What I was really excited about was seeing Isaac, and maybe even trying to talk to him for the first time. Oh, Anna, I thought to myself, you do know how to ramble on. I laughed out loud, and people gave me strange looks.

That afternoon, I went down to see Isaac, as I had planned, and saw him sitting there. I was overjoyed! I could see that he was drawing something new, and it made my heart race. What was he drawing now? Something even more incredible than the tree? I got closer, and saw that he actually had several drawings going on at the same time, and this time, I knew what they were instantly. He had drawn the steps that a tree seed undergoes when it grows. Each step was illustrated perfectly, and in the last, which he was just finishing, a small baby tree was being born from the earth. It was exactly like I had said earlier! It was Anna, the baby tree! It was a perfect match for the big Daddy tree I already had.

I was really excited. I realised I was sounding like a small child, but I didn't even care, I was that happy. What happened next caught me by surprise: Isaac brought his hand out to me. At first I was shocked, but when I got hold of myself, I realised that he must have been wanting the tree back, so I gave it to him. He placed it near the Anna tree, just as I had hoped he would. I began to cry. I missed my daddy so much. I wonder if Isaac even knew that he was having this effect on me. I watched as he started drawing on the Daddy tree again. I was surprised and stepped a little closer to see what he was doing. After just a few moments, he brought out an eraser.

I gasped out loud as he started to take away the incredible detail of the Daddy tree. But it got worse; what he added to the picture shocked me even more. He changed it, but not just a little. Isaac was KILLING the Daddy tree! I was heartbroken ... the beautiful Daddy tree was becoming a dead, lifeless husk of its former self. I cried, but this time they were tears of sorrow, something that I had not allowed myself to shed in a very, very long time.

Isaac placed the Daddy tree down again, with the Anna tree and all the other sapling drawings. I realised what he was trying to express: it was life. He was drawing the birth of life, the growing of life, and then, eventually, the death of life. Of course, it all made sense now; his parents and sister died in a fatal car accident. HE was the Anna tree, and the Daddy tree was his family. They were gone now, and now he was all alone.

I instinctively sat down next to him, and I hugged him. His body was cold against mine, but I knew that somewhere in there he must have felt my presence. Even if he didn't show it, which I didn't expect him to, and didn't need him to either. But the fact is. He did. His arms rose from his drawings and made their way, slowly, around my shivering body.

In a few days' time, the school year would finish, and I was worried I wouldn't see Isaac after that – something that I wouldn't have been able to stand. As if that couldn't have gotten any worse, right? Wrong. Isaac wasn't sitting at the bench when I went to check. Days passed, and eventually it reached a point where I thought he wasn't coming back. Five days till the end of the school year, then four, then three, then two, and eventually, there came a time when there was only a single day until the end of the year.

I started to panic when I arrived at school, praying to God that Isaac would be there, sitting at the bench again. But he wasn't. No, Isaac wasn't sitting at the bench in the afternoon. Instead, he was running towards me holding a piece of paper. Before I knew it, it was shoved in my hands, and I was reading it like you would read anything else. It was a ticket. A ticket to go on a plane. A plane that would take me to one of my favourite countries of all time: Italy.

"No. You're not going."

"But Mother! I love Italy more than anything!" I argued.

"I'm not letting you run off to some strange place with

some person I've never met before in my life!" she yelled back at me.

That last statement was enough to send me over the edge. If she had thought I had yelled at her before, then she never saw this coming. I shouted and shouted like I was insane, and this time, she didn't just listen. She was scared of me.

She stepped back slowly as I erupted in the lounge room. I tore at her like I was a predator, and she was my prey. If any expression a person can have on their face can mean that they are hurt, it was the one on my mother's face in that instant.

"YOU SAY THAT LIKE YOU DON'T DO THE EXACT SAME THING TO ME EVERY DAY! ALL NIGHT, YOU'RE OUT THERE WITH STRANGE MEN IN GODFORSAKEN PLACES! DON'T YOU DARE CRITICISE HOW I LIVE MY LIFE, YOU WASTE OF HUMAN FLESH!"

I ran from the house, my plane ticket to Italy firmly in my hand, and I didn't see my mother again for two whole years.

I sat with Isaac on the plane, and as I expected, Isaac didn't say a word, he didn't even show any sign of emotion, as I also expected. But I was feeling enough excitement for both of us. You see, I love Italy so, so much.

The buildings are just so unbelievably gorgeous, and would have to be the most spectacular thing I can imagine ever seeing. I was so excited, in fact, that I completely overlooked the fact that I was travelling to Italy with a guy I have never even spoken to, with no certain way to return. But the truth was that I didn't care. I already liked

Isaac more than I had liked practically anyone else I had ever met. I wanted to ask him so much. I mean, why was a guy who had just had his whole family die in a car crash flying with me to Italy? Did the elderly lady know? Who was she – his grandmother?

So many questions, and all I had to answer them was a tree, some saplings, and a face that told me nothing. Yet we were friends, now. In a strange way. The only friend I had ever really had, that was a person. When we were over Italy, Isaac started sketching what he could see below. The city of Florence was so gorgeous, I couldn't even believe my eyes at its spectacular presence. I knew enough Italian to get us by when it came to food and a place to stay.

Isaac, luckily for me, had brought money. Something that I had completely forgotten about, stupid girl. Once we had a place to stay and snacks to keep us going, we went out and explored the city of Florence. We didn't really have a plan of what we were going to do, but we didn't really need one. We sat near a river that went under a bridge, and spent the evening looking out at the buildings and people milling around. I was in awe, and I'm sure Isaac could see it on my face. But his face was still blank and expressionless, even as he sketched the city, in perfect detail. Not a single brow tensed, and he showed no sign of ... anything. His hand moved, but that was about it.

As we slept, two things were predominant in my mind: we were going to Venice tomorrow, my favourite city ever. And secondly, Isaac. Why did he bring me here to explore this beautiful place? Does he consider me his friend too? I was pretty sure he did; after all, he shared his trees with me, and every time he finished a part of his Florentine sketches, he would show me, and wait for my reaction.

"That's brilliant," I would reply with a smile.

Most of the time I would speak to him, knowing that he would be listening, and so I chatted into the shadows throughout the night, before we eventually slept.

"My name is Anna, by the way, just in case you didn't know. I really like your name: Isaac. This is such a beautiful city, don't you think?"

The only response was the sound of heavy breathing as he slept.

"Well, Anna, it's time to sleep, I think." And so I did, dreaming of the morning, when we would travel to Venezia.

I was woken in the middle of the night by screaming. What was going on? I jumped out of bed and turned on the light, expecting someone being murdered or some thief making away with someone's purse. But the cause of the screaming was nothing like that: it was Isaac.

He was twisting and turning in his sheets, yelling out in pain and anguish. I looked at his face; it was the first time I had seen any emotion on his face since he started drawing the Daddy tree. It was incredible; I just stood there watching, until sense got the better of me and I made the decision to help him. I shook him awake. He was sweating and breathing heavily. I made him sit up and got him a glass of water.

After a few minutes, he began to calm down. He lay on his bed, and his features slowly relaxed back to the way they had been the night before. We didn't bother going back to sleep, and instead decided to get up and go to Venice in the early morning. We arrived, and it

WAS beautiful. More beautiful than I had ever thought. The architecture was sensational! But my mind was on other things. Isaac and his screaming, the answers to the questions that still eluded me, and I realised that I was in a place very, very far from home.

Isaac sat in front of me as I curled up in a ball. He sketched the buildings as I examined them, with only half of my heart taking in the awesomeness of where I was. The thing was that I didn't know what we were going to do, where would we go next? But Isaac answered that question for me.

Later that evening, after we had had our pasta for dinner, Isaac passed me another ticket. This time, we were going to England. Why? I still didn't get it. And where did Isaac get all the money from to do this? Did he inherit that much money? And did he intend the two of us to live together, forever, without finishing our educations? I brought all of this up with him in that moment, sitting near a Venetian canal, but he didn't reply: I wasn't surprised.

I was restless on the plane trip this time, and I played around with my thumbs and tapped the ground. The man in front of us turned to me and asked me to be quiet. I apologised, and he rolled his eyes at me. I looked over at Isaac, but he still wasn't doing anything. Perhaps he never would.

As we were coming into England, Isaac started sketching from the window as he had in Italy. However, this time, there was a commotion on the back of the plane. I could hear arguments, and raised voices. I wondered what was going on, so I looked back. There was a man in a suit, who must have been a business man of some type, and he was obviously complaining about something. I was just about to start ignoring and go back to watching Isaac, but something happened then that caught my eye.

Another man in a suit joined the business man, and the two of them were getting uncomfortably close to the woman they were arguing with. It reminded me of the men back at home that had tried to get me to do things with them that I didn't want to. I frowned angrily, forcing myself to continue watching and not just run up and hit the men.

They forced the lady into a compartment, and the group of figures went silent. I couldn't hear anything now, and a child was screaming and crying behind Isaac and I. Its parents tried to calm it down, but that didn't work quite as they had planned it to.

I was getting frustrated now, and decided to just go and check this out myself. I stood, giving Isaac one short, reassuring look, and then made my way to the back of the plane. I made eye contact with each person as I walked along the aisle. I was almost near where the suited men had been, but was stopped by another man in a suit that had met me halfway down the aisle.

"What are you up?" the man said rudely as I reached his position.

"I'm just going to check something out. Not that it's any of your business," I responded.

"I think you had better return to your seat. Now."

And I didn't have much of a choice from that point. The man grabbed me and shoved me back into my seat, next to Isaac. I yelped as he did so, and many onlookers frowned up at him. But there wasn't much they could do, because a voice came over the speaker in that very instant. It wasn't the pilot.

"Excuse me, passengers. We apologise for the inconvenience, but this aircraft has been seized for purposes of international security. Please stay seated while we ensure your safety."

The plane then proceeded to land. The voice had sounded menacing; I didn't like the feel of all this. And neither did Isaac; in fact, Isaac stood, with a frown on his face. That's right – a frown, on Isaac's face. I was stunned. Isaac was showing some kind of emotion for the first time. But the surprises didn't end there. Isaac grabbed my arm, and yanked me towards the plane's exit. I gasped at his strength and forcefulness, but wasn't complaining when I looked back to see all three men in black suits running towards us.

"There they are!" they yelled out, but Isaac had already gotten me to the exit.

The issue was that it had been sealed closed. I panicked. But then the lady who the men had been harassing came over the speaker.

"I've opened the door! Run! Run! They're lying."

The voice was followed by the sound of a gunshot. Someone had shot her. I never knew if any of the other passengers had left the plane, because Isaac had taken the opportunity given by the air hostess immediately: racing off the plane, past the aircraft workers, past the airport, taking me over a fence at the edge of the airstrip. I had never moved so quickly before in my life.

We found our way into London after about an hour. Isaac gave me money, a look of urgency now on his face. I took the money and got us a place to stay for a while; the fact that everyone spoke the same language as me here made things easier.

When we were safely inside, I collapsed on a bed, and turned on the TV. The incident was on the news. Apparently it had been a group of men trying to collect hostages to bribe the government to give them money. I would never understand how someone could be so desperate for cash that they would put someone through something like that. Isaac sat out on the balcony overlooking the city and sketched. We stayed there until the evening. Isaac sketched, and I just lay there trying to clear my head. When he had finished, he came and showed me his sketches. I smiled; they were all amazing.

He brought life to the city on a piece of paper, and it occurred to me that we were in an incredible place. I went out to sit with him. I spoke to him about everything that had happened, and he looked out onto the city, quite obviously pondering every sentence I muttered.

It was then that I realised we hadn't had anything to eat, so I went out to get some food for the two of us. When I returned, he smiled up at me as I sat down, and as a result, I looked back at him for probably longer then was necessary. Then he laughed! He actually laughed! I was so surprised and thrilled that I giggled like an idiot.

After we had eaten, we sat together in silence, both of us grinning, and admiring the view. Any questions or fears that I had had over the past few weeks were completely gone as we sat there together, holding hands as the sun passed below the horizon.

We slept, and this time I wasn't woken by screaming in the morning. Isaac slept perfectly, and when I woke up first, I looked across and saw that Isaac was smiling as he slept. Only you, Anna, I thought to myself, only you could have this happen to you.

Over the next few weeks, Isaac and I travelled to lots of different places, each more fascinating and exciting as the last. I tried to keep a journal of everything that happened, keeping particular emphasis on his behaviour, which, as we explored some of the most interesting locations the world had to offer, changed dramatically. Isaac still didn't talk, at all, but he would smile and laugh and have a thoughtful expression every now and again, and it was exciting.

I thought over everything we had been through. How he had interested me from the very beginning, how we had hugged when he showed me his tree drawings (we hug a lot now), how he had invited me on this amazing adventure around the world. At first, I had had doubts; I mean, I barely knew him, really. But now, now I really felt that this was the most amazing holiday I had ever had, with one of the most amazing individuals I had ever met.

Isaac was my best friend. The most amazing friend a girl could ever have. He saved my life back in England! He got me out of that plane without sparing a single ounce of effort. He really cared for me, and I really cared for him. Maybe one day, he might regain the ability to speak, and then our relationship can thrive even more!

I bought the journal that I have been writing in while we were in Egypt. Egypt was incredible … I mean, amazing. We went to see the pyramids, which was easily one of the most astounding experiences of my life. Not even Isaac could help being open-mouthed at the sight of it. I giggled when I saw his face; it was priceless.

I was a bit scared when we started flying again, but Isaac hugged me whenever I looked worried. He started trying to tell me things through drawing. He drew me and him together a lot. Even though he could only see himself in mirrors, he was still able to draw the two of us in exact detail in the places we visited. It just convinced me even more than ever that he was a genius. I didn't think he would be able to do anything more amazing than that. But I was wrong.

Isaac took me to see the Himalayas, and when we got there, not only was he able to draw them in amazing detail, but it was almost as if the mountains were there on the page. He had this amazing way of making things appear the size they are in reality, but on the page. Like he did with the Daddy tree. The Himalayas were incredible, and for the first time I understood the power of nature.

For thousands of years we have built things, and nothing we have created matches the power and might of some of the earth's natural wonders. By the time we reached the Great Wall of China, we had so many drawings that Isaac had to buy a bag for them all. It reminded me of when Miranda had tried to make me carry a bag around with me. But this time, it had a practical use.

The Great Wall also reminded me of how I had felt when Miranda had died. The Wall itself was an amazing monument. But the reason it was built, to keep people out, and the knowledge that millions of people were thrown under its foundations to die was hard to think about. It occurred to me that human history is filled with great wonders, but also great tragedy and irony. I was learning more about the world then I ever could have at school. I then had a moment of realisation: it had been a full year since Isaac and I left to Italy. That meant that I had missed out on a year of school. No one knew where I was. Oh Anna ...

I woke up one morning to Isaac drawing in the corner of our hotel room. I yawned loudly, and pouted, hoping he would notice and think I was cute. But he didn't turn from his work, so I hopped over to see what he was up to. He was drawing something that I knew very, very well. It was the Eiffel Tower. We were going to Paris!

I couldn't help myself from feeling all giggly and girly about a boy taking me to Paris. Even though I usually wasn't into all of that romantic stuff. We caught the plane to Paris and we were away.

Isaac sat smiling through the whole flight, and didn't even take a moment to draw anything. I was extremely excited. Possibly more than I had ever been before in my life. I was feeling so bubbly and there was a feeling in my stomach that I had never felt before ... I was looking around, wondering how much longer I had to wait, when I had to go to the bathroom. I hugged Isaac and strutted off.

As I came back from the toilet, however, I saw something that confused everything I felt up until this point. Sitting on the plane. A few seats back from where we were. Was Mr. Spark. I returned to my seat next to Isaac, and faked a smile so he didn't know something was wrong. What is he doing here? I asked myself. I was confused as to what to do now. Should I go speak to him? He was the man who changed my life forever! But I hadn't spoken to him for years now ... he might not even remember me. In the end, I decided to just leave it, and get on with my trip with Isaac ... to Paris.

We got off the plane, and for the most part, I felt the excitement start to build again. This was such a stereotype. So much so that it was a little daggy. But it was cute anyway, and I liked it. We did what we always did: we got a room together, tried out the local cuisine, and spent some time exploring and sketching.

Paris was a really, really cool city. But it also had a dark side. Its history was very much barbaric at times, with many wars and the like, and security in Paris today was very high. But that didn't take away from the awesomeness of it all.

It was the same with the Great Wall; its history didn't take away from its utter awesomeness. Perhaps that's what Isaac saw in me, as well. Maybe, even though I've been through a lot. Felt a lot of pain. He still sees that I'm good. And I suppose I feel the same for him. His family died with him right beside them, and as a result, he doesn't talk, and only recently became able to speak, but I still think he's amazing. Who else can draw like him? For every memory we've had together, he has a drawing.

All across the world, we have had moments that he has been able to track with his spectacular drawing abilities. I guess in life you have to look at the positives in order to see the world in any sort of positive way. Isaac taught me that. Maybe I taught him the same. Isaac took me to a spot near the Eiffel Tower – it was astounding. He brought out his image of it, and improved it to meet his massively high standard.

We sat there for a while, under the Eiffel Tower, holding hands, and each other, and he looked at me in a way that let me know that he recognised everything we had been through together as well. I was cold, very cold, so he gave me his jacket. Everything just progressively became more and more stereotypical, and it was wonderful.

He drew for a while, I wasn't sure what of, but I didn't mind. Eventually he showed me: it was a picture of me, I looked very warm and comfortable in the picture, and above it was a question mark. I laughed, and then tried to contain myself, but resorted to giggling instead, which made him smile.

"Yes, thank you, I'm warm," I said, still giggling. "What about you, are you warm?" I asked, suddenly concerned.

He shrugged. Aww. I snuggled up to him to try to warm him up, I'm not sure if I succeeded, but he was grinning, so I guess that was something. I wasn't really expecting what came next. I suppose I should have, because it was the thing you would expect to happen in this kind of situation. But yeah, I'm a bit thick, so I didn't work it out until ... it happened.

Isaac kissed me. I was so shocked that I just lay there on him with my eyes wide open, gawking. I tried to relax, and I'm not sure how that went, but when we stopped, he was grinning, so I don't think I did anything too wrong. I was so red. I just giggled and got redder and redder as he took me back to our hotel.

The next day Isaac and I headed to a little shop that had lots of little knick knacks and stuff. I loved it, and starting running around and grabbing things that I wanted. Isaac would just smile at me as I pranced about. When my hands were full, I went over to him and gave him my things to hold while I went to get more.

"I love you," said Isaac.

I stood there, stunned. In the end all I could do was

turn around and keep shopping. But I made sure I looked back and smiled, just so he didn't think I was upset. As I grabbed lots more stuff, I thought about what he had just said. I couldn't believe it. He loved me. As in LOVE. I couldn't believe it. Not only that, but he just SPOKE. He NEVER speaks. That means that his first words since the accident were telling me that he loves me.

I grabbed more and more things that I liked, thinking of how to respond, but I just couldn't rationalise anything. What to say! I mean, were we going to be together forever now? Could what I say now ruin it all?

I turned around to see Isaac writing something in a little notebook he had picked up. What was he doing now? I could hardly breathe, what was going on? I didn't know where to look, what was the right thing to do? Oh my holy God, what was I meant to do? I was so happy. So incredibly happy. I turned to say something to Isaac, but he gave me a piece of paper. I needed to say what I needed to say, so I stuffed the note in my pocket for later; right now, I needed to say something in response to what he said! I turned away from him again, still not knowing what to do.

Come on, Anna … just say, "I love you too."

Yes, that's what I knew I needed to do. I turned around to say to Isaac what I needed to say to him. But he was already saying something to me.

"Run!"

In that moment there was a gunshot. I saw Isaac fall to the ground in front of me. I screamed. I looked up to see who had shot him. I looked up to see someone I knew. I looked up to see someone I thought I knew very, very well. Someone I admired. It was Mr. Spark. Mr. Spark had shot Isaac.

Isaac was dead.

I ran. I screamed. I ran faster and faster. I screamed louder and louder. I reached the hotel and fell to the ground crying. I locked myself inside the room and I cried for hours. I didn't care why this was happening, or what I should do under these circumstances. All I cared about was that Isaac was gone. Isaac had been taken from me by a man I thought was the best man I had ever met. I cried until there was nothing left inside of me. I was dead to the world for a very long time. I don't know how many days passed by before I realised something: Isaac had given me a note. I opened it quickly, and it read:

Anna,

I want to thank you for everything you have done for me.

You changed my life in ways that you can't ever imagine.

When I first saw you, watching me as I drew, I didn't feel anything, I was hollow. Ideas came out onto the paper, but I didn't FEEL them.

But you changed that. You made me feel again. You made me see the world as more than just a chaotic place of vulgarity.

This morning, I left all of our drawings on the table. Please keep them. They are for you, and only you.

I'm sorry, for I have kept things from you over the past

year that you deserved to know. But if I hadn't kept them from you, we wouldn't have shared the time we did together.

I don't know the details myself, but my father worked with some people. Important people that do important things. That's all he ever told me. My father discovered a plot that another group had formed to steal a massive amount of money from the world's governments. Because he was the one that discovered this plot, he and my family were executed.

Except I survived. I wasn't meant to, but I did.

And I brought you into all of this. They thought that you were Miranda, that you had survived the crash as well. They've been following us. And all this time I've tried to keep them off our track. They found us in London, but we lost them. But as you probably know by now, it was in vain. They found us. I knew when we arrived in Paris. Their leader, Montgomery Spark, was following us personally. And by now he will have killed me.

But don't worry, you aren't in danger. My dad taught me well, I made sure that he thought that Miranda was caught back in China. He thinks we're all dead now. And we are. But the information is still in the hands of my dad's colleagues. They will be caught, Anna. You don't need to worry ever again, their plot will be foiled, and you are safe.

Again, please keep the drawings.

I love you so much,

Isaac

A YEAR LATER I RETURNED home. My mum and I made up. I understood why she made my life hell: she missed Dad as much as I did, she just didn't know how to control her frustration. I told her everything. Showed her all of the pictures, and told her about the many beautiful things I had seen while on my adventure with Isaac. Mum died a few months later. And now I'm all alone. But that's not true. One is never alone. There are always new stories to explore, or new messages from loved ones that you didn't quite see. One time, for example, I was looking through all of Isaac's drawings, when I noticed letters on all of them. I placed all of them together, side by side, and filtered all of the letters out. It was a message. It said, "All of these places: they are so, so beautiful, just like you."

And so I finally figured out why Isaac took me around the world with him: To show the world what he already saw in me.

My name is Anna. But you don't really need to know that. This isn't really a story about me. It's a story about a friend of mine. It was a friend that came out of nowhere and changed my life forever. His name was Isaac. And I will love him forever.

At this point, Opaulde's writings, unfortunately, fall into disarray. It began with small things such as the misspelling "Italy" which is most likely a reference to the country "Etarli" and escalated to a point where each word had no relation to the next. I believe this was a period of madness on his part.

—Darcy

Chapter Five

O paulde has a few more tales to tell. Following some, he has a period of philosophy. I may be mistaken but it seems as if Opaulde is experimenting with emotions. I'm not certain he believes everything he writes.

—*Darcy*

The Erroneous Jubilee

I T HAS COME TO MY attention in recent years that the world I love and cherish is not quite so well known as I (as a child, mind you) had at first believed. In fact, reality is many times larger than, I think, any of us take the time to even consider. That is one of the purposes of this tale, to sprinkle a little perspective on reality, and in turn, inspire interest on the subject. The second purpose of the tale, and

I will try to be brief (for what is a story if it cannot speak for itself?), is to explore, I suppose, the darker side of the flowers, the celebrations and fairy tales. That is not to say that this has not been done before; however, this tale has somewhat of a personal touch when it comes to myself. What is a story without some level of experience to back it up? But don't get me wrong, when I say 'experience', I do not mean the decade-long research into various fields of science, I mean emotional experience. The experience that comes with feeling something, and taking something from an experience that changes the way you see things in the future.

Now, I find nothing more annoying than an extremely long introduction. I'm sure more than a few of us have skipped the ... nonessential ... parts of a novel to reach the meaty bits. So my introduction to the tale I am about to tell ends now, with just one final set of statements, so that you don't run head first into the story without some understanding: imagine a place you have been to recently; picture it in your mind, not just a room, but an entire town, city, country, anywhere you have been that you can imagine and, preferably, have been to. Now I want you to empty this place, so that it is nothing but a cask. A completely empty place, waiting for ideas to clump together to create a story. If your place is considerably large, you might want to minimalise a little, because the tale begins in this place, this empty place. An empty, but familiar place. A place with a manor house, and that is where we are going.

There could not possibly have been anything in the entire world that could have annoyed Kai Winterbaubles more at that moment than the bickering of his Aunty

Ferelda in the dining room.

This frustration was amplified by the fact that his mother, as always, was making it her job to suck up to Aunty Ferelda as much as is humanly possible. Kai's mother was not a bad mother, he wouldn't say, but there was something about her that always made Kai wonder where her priorities lay.

Her name was Lady Antara Winterbaubles, respected wife of the great Lord Fredrick Winterbaubles, but then again, all the fancy names and all never really meant anything to Kai, who preferred to be outside, with his animal friends.

The reason that the Lord and Lady of Winterbauble Manor were so keen for Aunty Ferelda's approval was due to the immense power the mistress held over Winterbauble Manor and the rest of the land. She had shares in every business out there, and could easily make the Winterbaubles rich ... or destroy them.

Kai had been told to stay in his room until the talks came to a close, but he had other ideas. This wasn't the first time he had had to leave the main building of the manor ... unnoticed ... but there was just one problem. Kai had always climbed out his window, onto the ledge, lowering himself onto a rather steady hanging set of pot plants, before hanging down on the window ledges below and landing after a short leap onto the bench on the side of the path. The issue, however, was that the set of pot plants had been taken away, for reasons Kai was not sure of, and felt it best not to ask anyway. This left a massive gap in his usual climbing routine. The climb was now practically unachievable.

This was so typical, nothing ever seemed to go right for Kai; he was the one son of his seven siblings that seemed to have no place. All of them: Harod, Henry, Harry, Hordan, and his sisters, Hesla, Harriet and Harley, all had some amazing task that they were doing for Mother and Father. They were loved, and were given money for their 'troubles'. And, as always, Kai was left out, alone, he didn't get anything for it, and no work was ever even offered to him, and he knew why. It was because of how he looked.

All of his brothers and sisters were all stunningly beautiful and handsome, especially Hordan. Everyone loved Hordan, he was the role model for all the children of the town, the brave son of the great Lord Fredrick! How could Kai ever compete? But Kai tried to forget about it, about how he was burnt when he was born.

His mother had been careless; well, that was just a little harsh, the house had been attacked after all, and Kai had been, in the chaos, left alone on a table. There had been nothing plain to the eye that would have placed the infant in any danger whatsoever; in fact, you might say that, considering the manor was being attacked, leaving the baby there was a wise thing to do. Kai had learnt afterwards that the manor had been attacked by a ruthless gang of bandits and cutthroats that, as for now, remained unidentified, although their work had been well known over the past few years, attacking caravans and small settlements outside of the manor.

But this was different, the bandits had grown in confidence, and had made the ambitious decision to raid Winterbauble Manor. The Lady Antara and the servants were captured almost the moment they exited the manor to investigate. Kai's brothers Harry, Henry and Harod were all sent to their rooms. Harriet, his only sister at the time, was told to do the same by her father.

Lord Fredrick approached the leader of the bandits as his men filled the manor, taking positions throughout the area. It had seemed to the servants, and indeed, the Lady Antara, that all hope of a successful defence had been crushed. It was at that moment that the five-year-old Hordan left his room to investigate; he walked down the hallways that contained the bedrooms, and was just about to walk down the stairs, towards the entrance to the manor, when he heard the cries of a baby.

Filling with realisation, Hordan ran towards the doorway to Kai's place of birth, and upon entry, saw the baby lying there on the table. Hordan picked up the newborn Kai, pleading to the child to be quiet, as to not draw attention to them; however, he simply grew louder after every second.

The bandits had now secured the lower level of the manor, taking in any remaining servants, including the chef. They began to climb the stairs, and as Hordan watched several of them stomping up to the upper level, one bandit heard Kai wailing.

Hordan panicked to find a hiding spot, and as any child might, he chose the table. Conveniently, there was a table cloth hiding the baby and Hordan from sight, and as Hordan forced Kai to be silent by placing his own fist inside the baby's mouth, the bandit entered the room. Hordan could smell him, he had the most appalling, dirty smell Hordan had ever smelt, and what was worse, he knew exactly where the children were hiding.

But this bandit wanted to play with them, so he

wandered slowly, his muddy boots trudging through the previously clean carpet. He called out to them, mocking their innocence, while turning over various objects and saying things such as, "Oh! They aren't there ... I wonder where they're hiding ..."

Harod held his breath and tried very hard not to exist. What if Father had been taken away by the bandits ... and what if they ... what if they were taking things from HIS room! Hordan could not let this happen; he could hear the bandit getting closer and closer, and knew that any time now, he and his little brother would be caught. Hordan's heart was beating extremely fast, he knew he had to do something, but he was just far too scared. He was frozen stiff, because he had always had nightmares about this kind of thing.

Men coming for him in the middle of the night, and although it was not night at the time, it felt like it. It felt like he was wandering down from his room, through the dark hallways, down the stairs, and into the kitchen ... in the middle of the pitch black night. And once he had his snack, he would sprint back into his room, so that the scary things could not find him. But this time it was real, it was REAL, and it made him feel like crying, that his worst fears and nightmares were coming true. And no blanket would help him. What he wouldn't have done at that time to return to the dark, dark kitchen, where all of his fears were in his head only – and his head alone.

The bandit came over to the table where Hordan and his little brother resided, and Hordan went dead still. A tear ran down his cheek as he remembered the joy he had had at the news that his brother would soon be born, and now he held him in his own arms, his last hope of a life other than that of slavery to the bandit gang. Silence seemed to fall for what felt like a very ... very long time. But Hordan knew that it would come soon, the moment where the bandit would pull back the tablecloth, and do unspeakable things to him and his brother.

It happened, and when it did, the bandit reached down under the table, grabbing what would have been Hordan's collar, if it hadn't been for his absence at that point, because Hordan had taken Kai and jumped from under the table, making a run for the door, his heart racing and bubbling at high temperatures in his chest.

Hordan ran for the stairs, the bandit right behind him, frustrated and angry at the small child that had thwarted him. Hordan went for the manor door, but bandits at the entrance were already watching him; he side tracked into the lounge room where he slammed the door closed behind him. He then ran over to the window, placing his little brother in a chair; he was trying to open it so that he could escape from the bandits that were already charging towards the lounge room door.

Hordan had tears in his eyes as he failed, because he did not have the key that was needed to open the window. The bandit leader smashed through the door, running towards the child at the window. In utter panic, Hordan reached for his little brother, but at the same time, the bandit lord grabbed Hordan around the waist, and as Hordan struggled in fear, Kai was flung from his arms, into the fire place. The bandit released Hordan in shock at the sight of the infant screaming as he entered the flames. Hordan barely hesitated to grab his brother out of the fire, and it probably saved his life, but the damage was still serious, and as Hordan looked into the lounge room doorway to meet the eyes of his father, bloodied sword in his hand, terror was born on both of their faces.

The raid did not last long after that. Lord Fredrick cut down the bandit leader before tending to his sons, and without their leader, the bandits ran for the hills. Hordan's frantic escape into the lounge had distracted the bandit leader enough for Fredrick to free the servants and his wife, and take back the manor, mostly thanks to the death of the bandit lord. The manor would have returned to normal, if it weren't for the fact that Kai had been badly burnt. Many doctors were called to Kai's bedside, and in the end, after months of healing, the boy was left with no permanent injury, except for the scorching on his face and shoulders. This was why, he had told himself, he was always considered to not be as good as his brothers and sisters. Hordan had been praised as a hero and was said to be "just like his father", and it was true; Hordan had saved Kai's life, and perhaps even the lives of everyone at the manor, but Kai was the one who had to suffer all his life as a result.

Kai grew ever more frustrated at the voices of his Aunty Ferelda and his mother, and made the decision to try to climb through the window despite the absence of the hanging pot plants.

He opened the window, and was greeted by nice weather: no wind, and a little bit of sunlight. He climbed out onto the ledge, lowering himself so that he was hanging from the windowsill. What he essentially had to do now was very difficult; he would have to drop down to the next window ledge from a height of two to three metres and manage to grasp the ledge without falling. He had always grabbed onto the supports of the hanging pot plants in order to lower himself that extra metre or two, but this time he could not do that.

Kai hung there for a long time, trying to build the courage to drop down, but he never found it. It wasn't until his arms started to ache that he knew he had to do something. He tried pulling himself up, but he had lost too much strength. Before he could do anything about it, he lost his grip on the ledge and began to fall down to the ground. His heart stopped and his throat made a strange gasping sound as he tried to grab onto the window ledge below. Kai made a split-second decision to bring his body into the window itself, and as he did, he landed awkwardly within the frame, slamming his head and scratching his knees on stone. But that was the least of his problems; his efforts had resulted in the smashing in of a part of the window. He knew he would be in a lot of trouble for that, but he decided that this wasn't the time to worry about such things, because he had made it, and with a momentary gulp at the smashed window, he jumped down onto the bench below.

Kai ran across the path onto the lawn, and over to the fence, where his friend, Cal, was waiting for him. Winterbauble Manor had a farm, and Cal, as well as being Kai's friend, also happened to be a sheep. Kai said hello, before jumping over the fence, and running with Cal over to their favourite tree. Kai had met Cal near this very same tree years ago, when Kai had escaped the house to get away from Harley's crying, when she was a baby. Cal was grazing near the tree as Kai sat there, playing with the grass. He had eventually fallen asleep under the tree, and Cal, realising, came over to him, and ate the grass Kai had been playing with. This repeated several times, and each time, Kai barely noticed that Cal was there. Cal would graze, and when Kai fell asleep, most of the time after eating cake or some other snack, Cal would come over and eat some grass.

One day, however, all the grass had almost been eaten, because Kai had continued to pull it out of the ground, and Cal would eat it with ease. So when Cal came over and expected freshly pulled grass, he was disappointed, and a little angry, because there was none left. Cal started prodding Kai in an attempt to wake him up, trying to discover why he had not pulled out any grass for him. When Kai finally woke, he screamed, and almost had a heart attack from the fright of waking up to see a sheep poking away at him.

The sheep stepped back at this, and stood there waiting. Kai sat still for a while, wondering what in the world this sheep wanted from him. Eventually he stood up and tried to walk away, but Cal just followed on behind him. Soon they came to a spot that Kai had never been to before, close to where he knew there was a forest.

Kai soon grew accustomed to the sheep following him around, and started expecting it as the days went by. Weeks later, when the sheep had followed him on several occasions, Kai sat down by a new tree that he had found on his walks, and, like he had before, started to pull out the grass. Cal reacted immediately, swooping in to eat the grass. Kai smiled, and said, "You like that, aye?"

After a decent amount of time of grass pulling, eating and feeding, Kai started to wonder what he should call his new friend. So to work it out he played a game. Kai would place blades of grass in the shape of letters on the ground, and whichever one the sheep ate first, would be the next letter in his name. The first time failed, the sheep simply stood over both the A and the B that Kai had made. The next time, he got lucky, and the sheep ate the letter C before D. So the sheep's name would start with C. Over the next few weeks, Kai tried again and again, but the sheep always sat, or lay, or stood on the letters, trampling them. In the end, Kai had to start the alphabet again, and, to his delight, the sheep finally ate another letter: the letter A. Over the next few days, Kai repeated this process, and eventually found himself with Y and Z again. This time, the sheep ate Z. But Kai didn't like the name Caz, so he decided that he would just have to make the decision himself, to save time. He decided on the name Cal.

"Hello Cal! I'm Kai!"

Cal, naturally, just continued to eat, and so it went on, for many weeks and months and years.

Lies

IT'S TRUE THAT LORD SHIRLEY is a little harsh, and maybe even cruel to us, but calling him evil is a bit of an overstatement. He always gives us pay, the work isn't all that difficult, and you get used to it after doing the same thing since you were five. I was brought up in Resemblarge, and was assigned to the Printing Presses when I was little, by Lord Fhug. Ever since, I have been under the supervision of Lord Shirley. I've learnt to get used to hearing, "Jordan! Wake up!" every morning at four o'clock, and then having to start my shift.

It's for the good of Resemblarge, because someone needs to make sure the daily notices are printed for display over the Visi-coms. How it works is, we are given a notice, and we pass it on down the never-ending line of workers (I am no. 678), and as each of us receives it, we copy it on our individual printing presses, and then pass the notice on. We then have to take our new notice down to the Visi-com terminal and place it in the display pockets, and the notice is carried out to a settlement within Resemblarge, where the notice is displayed on a massive Visi-com, that can be seen by all citizens in that District.

The notices usually contain orders for the workers of each District. The Printing Pressers and I are in the Central District of Resemblarge, where all communication is maintained, and where the Focus Building of High Lord Adrian is. I do this every day, and will until I am too old, when someone will replace me. Lord Shirley is in charge of the entire Sector of Printing Pressers, and maintains all communication with the other Districts. He is a very stressed man and shouts a lot, which is why a lot of people think he's evil. He has been known to punish rather violently, but I myself have never seen this.

Resemblarge is a huge building on the surface of the planet, the last refuge for organic life forms. Outside of Resemblarge there is nothing but toxic gases and dust storms. We work all day, in all the Districts, in every Sector across Resemblarge to ensure that everything keeps working normally. There are Districts responsible for oil, shields, metal maintenance, food creation, water purification, and the list goes on. Other than High Lord Adrian, no one within the Districts has much communication with one another; there isn't enough time to waste for that. But we trust High Lord Hadrian to keep things running.

One day, while I was working at the Presses, Lord Shirley came to my Leg of the Presses, screaming his head off, shouting about how he had too much to do.

"Can I help you, sir?" I asked instinctively.

"Hmph ..." he replied, thinking. "Yes, take this to the Focus Building for me. I don't have enough time, I'm running late, you see."

"Yes, sir!" The Focus Building? I was delivering to the Focus Building? I started walking up towards the massive steps that I had only ever seen from afar. I stared in awe at the hugeness of the building; it was larger then the rest of the District.

I entered through the door, and immediately, I was questioned. I responded simply that Lord Shirley had sent me to deliver a message straight to High Lord Adrian, and they let me pass.

Eventually I made my way into the Inner Sanctum, where I was told to enter the office of High Lord Adrian and wait for his arrival. I entered, and my heart skipped a beat as I realised I had been asked to deliver a message to the High Lord of Resemblarge ... of the entire planet. I stood near the desk that I assumed was his, and I waited. But nothing happened. I waited for what felt like hours, but still nothing.

Eventually curiosity got the better of me, and I walked over to the window. The view was incredible, I could see so much of the District, and I could see almost all of the Printing Presses ... hundreds ... lined up, printing, and I realised that there wasn't just one origin of the notices, but a massive, complex system of hundreds and hundreds of notices ... all going out to different Sectors, of different

Districts. How massive is Resemblarge? If this is just one District ... and there are all those notices ... I tripped backwards over the High Lord's chair, and searched the room with my eyes to see if anyone saw. There was no one there, thank God. On the High Lord's desk, I noticed his PC-OnD, which stands for Personal Communication-Omninet Device. I wanted to take a look so badly, to just glance at it, and I had been left in here for so long now, it wouldn't hurt to take just one tiny look.

I opened the PC-OnD, and was instantly shocked by what I saw. The High Lord's network systematics showed an entire bird's eye view of Resemblarge, every District and Sector, detailed with its industrial purpose. But that wasn't the most shocking thing. The network included more than just Resemblarge, it included an overview of the entire planet ... systems ... everywhere.

And one thing made me feel sick. On the planet's surface, there were cities ... places completely exposed to the outside air ... so many of them ... thousands ... the names were endless ... Paris ... Brussels ... London ... What were these places ... They went on and on ... Countries: Syria, Canada, Russia. And they were all outside of the Resemblarge and other District systems. All this time ... they had lied to us, we were working endlessly, believing that the world above was uninhabitable, when really we were just serving those above, for their convenience.

I dropped the PC-OnD on the desk, but High Lord Adrian saw me just before I had time to hide my tracks. But he didn't look mad, he just stood and grinned. He raised one arm in the air, moving his finger so that I could see a red light being emitted from a ring, he typed a number into a buckle on his shirt, '678' followed by the letter 'A', and I felt my heart stop. I fell to the ground.

"How did the delivery go, young man?" The voice was Lord Shirley's.

"Fine, sir. High Lord Adrian was waiting in his office. He sends his thanks," I say, and return to my Printing Press.

The figure takes the animal's pelt and returns to his village.

Opaulde has taken us all over the place at this point. It's natural to be confused for his mind is chaotic like the world he lives in. He continues to write about some of the things he has explored in fiction.

—Darcy

Chapter Six

'RIGHT' AND 'WRONG' ARE MANMADE concepts. They are completely relative to what perceives them. So, then, do we create an illusion of purpose so that we might stay sane? Or do we give into the pointlessness that existence may hold? Sometimes people are ignorant, but if all of us were aware of the truth, it would just lead to more chaos. But what of us who know? The ones who have the mind to ask the question. If everything is relative, what do WE do? What are WE to believe?

Well, I fear that the answer is simple, that there may not be an answer. The Universe was not made for us, we simply grew independently from natural evolution. In all truth, if I went out and murdered everyone, it would have no real significance. We as a species would perceive my actions as 'terrible' and 'horrible', but it would not affect anything of great significance.

Ah, but perhaps the answer lies there. What IS of great 'significance'? Nothing. Without us, that is. So, then, would it indeed be significant, if I were to kill millions of people, merely because something believes it to be? So we have an answer, in a way that tells us to believe what WE believe. Find our own truth. Thus, do we enter into a great conflict against those with different beliefs? I would hope not. I would like to see all Humans realise what I have stated above. NOT to give up on their beliefs. NOT to believe what I do. But simply as a guide ... a guide to what? Yes, I'm not quite sure what it would guide us to.

Mutual understanding? And perhaps something to convince others that primitive conflict, greed and corruption is not the answer. But, even IF this was possible, it would take too long, right? It will never happen in our lifetime. Well, I say, sow the seeds now, so that children of the future may climb a tree fully grown.

We are greedy and corrupted by power. For example, the Roman Empire used religion as a form of social governing. A way to control massive amounts of worshippers. Also, on a different subject. Through history, 'the smart ones' are kinda picked on by 'the cool ones'. Firstly I'd like to say, reasonably, we are the cool ones, and secondly, you have to ask yourself, who was famous? Leonardo da Vinci or Jimmy Bob the drunk gambler from the Roman Thieves Guild?

And, finally, back to what this is meant to be about, in response to such statements as: "While people have free will there can be NO peace." And that, "People are stupid."

There will always be obstacles while people have free will, but we should overcome them, not ignore them. To fight evil is to fight evil. To surrender to it is to serve it. How many people have spent their lives thinking that they can do nothing to help and just shouldn't bother? More than is calculable.

But such thoughts only serve the growing web of darkness that is the reason they gave up in the first place. This is our only life. Our only chance to act. So I conclude with a question. Are you going to give up at the only thing you may ever have?

I feel a story coming ...

If there is a God, why does he allow bad things to happen? Perhaps a God would have no compassion. Imagine that. A being more powerful than us in almost every way has no perspective of love, empathy or friendship. To me, this would make that being inferior. At least in one way—an important way.

At least to me.

The Master

"YA'LL KNOW WHY YE 'ERE den?" The man's breath corrupted the divine smells of the gardens; the tulips and roses, though spring it was, seemed to bow down dead in the presence of this yellow-toothed, crazy-haired brute. He was truly horrific. His mouth spat into the faces of the sailors in front of him.

"All but I sir ..." gulped a young boy from the back of the crowd that had gathered there to be a part of this expedition. "I have nowhere else to be sir ... nowhere to go ... it seems to make sense I travel with you."

The boy felt hundreds of eyes watching him; he sunk his eyes unseen beneath his golden hair, in an attempt to hide. But he knew he had to do this ... he couldn't go back.

The boy stood in painful silence, waiting for a response. He could taste the bitterness in the air. He could feel the burning eyes of the man at the front of the crowd.

"You ... a wimpy little kid like you ... wants to travel wit us, on a journey of such importance?"

"Importance..." the crowd whispered, slightly giggling.

The boy remembered the things that the wise man had taught him; holding the brand he had been given, he lost all the feelings of dread and public display. That was the old you ... you're different now, he told himself. He tried to find the man's weakness, a way to confront him, but he was small, skinny and would appear unwanted. His only advantage was his mind.

"I've been to Flannan Isle ... I know shortcuts, and secret places ... you need me."

There was silence. Then the man, eyebrows raised, slowly turned, and walked up the ramp, onto the ship. The boy tasted victory, and his blue eyes glistened in the sunlight. It had begun.

The vessel had not the room nor the supplies to sustain a crew of twenty-three. It was extremely small, and as the boy touched the wooden planks, they creaked and felt like they would fall apart at the lightest touch. The majority of the crew were about the deck, working as sailors do.

"Boy!" yelled the Captain. "Come here," and so he did.

The Captain was wearing a fine Captain's outfit, his face was clean, though he had many scars, and his fair brown hair was neatly placed, sticking out the sides of his hat.

The boy now stood just a few metres from the Captain, at the front of the ship.

"What is your name, boy?" His voice was almost ... kind. Fatherly, almost.

"My name is ..." he began, feeling comfortable in the Captain's presence, but then in seeing the first mate, he hesitated. It was the brute from before. "Alexander." he said.

"Well, my name is Captain Tenpin; this is my first mate, Growsly."

Alexander looked at Growsly; something was suspicious. He tasted something in the air, the smells of the sea began to intensify. The boy saw something in the Captain's eyes; it made him cautious. He leaned back on the banister; it was cold to touch and his face went numb under the sea breeze.

"Come with me," laughed Growsly. "I have some questions."

Alexander stood up straight and obeyed Growsly's orders, knowing all along that this was what was necessary.

Growsly sat on a small chair behind a wooden table in a room just off the cabins. Growsly had seen his brand, and had given him a bizarre look, which he ignored. Alexander watched, listened and felt, paying attention to everything, as the old man had taught him. The sounds of clanging metal echoed through the corridors as ornaments and treasure clattered in every corner. He saw candles that were burnt out and tasted age in the air. This ship was many years old; the crew, however, were neither old enough nor fierce enough to have owned this ship for all its life.

Sure, Growsly looked rough, but Alexander saw that he could have been outmatched by a mouse. He had barely even noticed when Alexander had tested his guard. It was weak, and unpolished. Alexander had struck him, in a fashion that would have passed as a trip, in order to test Growsly. If Alexander had have wished it, Growsly would be dead now, for there were many sharp objects laying around, and Alexander had no fear of death, nor in himself or others. Surely, he would feel some level of empathy, for he was human, but not enough to regret.

Growsly was a bad man, this he knew. But killing him was out of Alexander's interests. Growsly gave an evil look; Alexander pretended to look scared. When Growsly leaned in, Alexander would lean out, but his mind was always clear.

Finally, Growsly said, "What do you know 'bout Flannan Isle?"

The boy turned his head. "Everything," he said with a glance in Growsly's direction. "What do YOU know about Flannan Isle?"

Growsly smirked at Alexander's response. "You listen 'ere! You gonna tell me everything you know, or you won't see the sky again! Understood?"

"You would kill me?" Alexander played.

"You afraid of deff, kid?" mocked Growsly.

"No, I die now, die later, it's of no significance."

Growsly scowled, and hunched over the table with threat in his eyes.

Alexander saw the perfect opportunity to win this confrontation. "But ... if I die later ... then I'll tell you everything."

Growsly had had enough.

Alexander smiled to himself as he was led to the Captain by Growsly. Alexander could see in Growsly's eyes, that the first mate thought that the Captain would punish, torture and bring the information forth from the him.

No, thought Alexander, I have the Captain on my side ... I could feel it ... but why? Why would he have pity for me? The ship was now far out at sea, and Captain Tenpin was in his private quarters. What a perfect place to be taken.

"So, boy," began the Captain once he and Alexander were seated, and Growsly long gone. "I'll give you a choice ..." The Captain said this with a surprisingly, however, not surprising for Alexander, high level of decency. "Tell me everything you know, and WE, that's right, YOU AND I, will share the secrets of Flannan Isle, together."

Alexander grabbed an apple from the bowl on the Captain's desk, tasting it with a great crunch and talking with his mouth full. "Sounds like a plan ... however ... why? Why me?" He placed the apple down on the hard wood, and addressed the Captain with stubborn seriousness.

Alexander held onto the taste of fruit, and silently smelt the scents, perfumes and flowers that had been especially obtained for the quarters, in the interest of the Captain's leisure. Alexander swallowed, holding his hands in his lap and watching the Captain from what felt like a room away. Their eyes locked. I have him.

Suddenly, Alexander was shocked when the Captain smiled and said, "Why you? You carry the brand of my master."

Alexander's thoughts travelled back to his days with the old man. He had taught him everything he knew. Alexander was once a street kid; he couldn't talk to adults, not to mention other children. He lived his own life, stole his food, and made no contact with people. When he was five ... or was it six ... seven perhaps, he ran away from his mother, for fear that she would eat him. He lived on the streets, barely surviving for three years. When one day, the old man saw him, and took him in. He seemed to understand him, instantly. He was a father, he was the Master.

The next few years changed Alexander's life. He grew, physically and mentally. He became one of the Master's students. A learner of knowledge. He was Alexander: the Master's student.

Captain Tenpin grinned, showing his brand to the boy. "I, too, was taught by the old man. It seems you were rather quick to learn ... it took me many years to realise the significance of what he had taught me." He trailed off, his eyes looked dreamy.

"How," Alexander began, "did the master find you?"

The Captain stared into space for some time, perhaps trying to remember, or wanting to forget.

Alexander, while waiting for the answer, took his time to think things through. This was an old ship, obviously once owned by a great crew for many years, certainly not the crew that were here now. The Captain, Growsly and ten others had been on the ship when it had arrived; the others, including Alexander, had joined at the docks. The Captain was a student of the Master, as was he, and was travelling to Flannan Isle, likely for the same purpose as he was; however, from his stories, it was obvious that Tenpin had taken a far longer amount of time to do as the Master ordered. Five, maybe ten years, it must have taken him to follow the old man's wishes, as Alexander had without question.

"I was a wealthy boy ... had everything..." the Captain began, "but it wasn't enough for me ... I wanted more." The Captain smiled a private smile.

"When did HE make an appearance?" Alexander questioned further.

"When my parents were murdered ... I threw everything away ... bought this boat ... hoped to die at sea." Tenpin's face dropped. "But then ... one day ... I came to shore to visit my parents' graves, and the old man was there. This repeated for years, he visited when I did, spoke to me, tried to help me be strong, to live on. Then one day, he took me to his house, he fed me, not with food, for he had none. He fed me with knowledge ... he gave me love, when no one else would." Captain Tenpin grinned.

Alexander grinned. So the ship was not always in this crew's hands ... yes, it was far older than that. Alexander wondered how the Captain had reacted to the Master's request. When he asked, he had his answer.

"What happened ... you know?" Alexander inquired.

The Captain looked panicked. "No ... nothing happened! NOTHING HAPPENED!" Tenpin leapt from his chair and flung himself out the doorway.

Alexander sat there ... in the darkness ... alone.

Alexander sat there, thinking. He had a good idea of what was going on. But he wondered of the ship's history. How many times had it been to the infamous Flannan Isle? Who were those who owned it before Tenpin? And what of before them? How many had travelled in search of omniscience, as he and the Captain were, and how many more, not for knowledge, but for fame and fortune?

Alexander pondered for a long time: hours, in fact. The old boat swayed in the ocean, calming and relaxing. Alexander thought of his childhood, the one he never had. He would go down to the river with his parents and collect berries, and skip and sing. His parents would call him inside for the evening meal, and they were happy. But that never happened. He never met his father, and his mother only kept him for food and labour. His dreams were fantasies ... and that was all. Suddenly, from the deck, Alexander heard cries of terror.

"HE'S DEAD!" came the voices of the sailors. "HE'S DEAD!" Alexander listened from the Captain's private quarters. He listened for a name. There, that was it. "GROWSLY IS DEAD!"

Alexander wondered why, and sure enough came the cry.

"A KNIFE! IN HIS BACK! GROWSLY IS DEAD!"

Alexander heard Tenpin's voice as well.

"Who?" The Captain said with disgust.

"IT WAS HIM!"

"NO!"

"YES! IT WAS HIM!"

"WHO?"

"HIM!"

"BUT YOU SAID HIM!"

"IT WAS BOTH OF THEM!"

"NEVER!"

It went on for a great deal of time. Arguments between the crew. Back and forth came the screams and shouts of protest. Alexander had a feeling, he knew, that the ship had arrived. They had arrived at Flannan Isle. The curse had reached the ship, and they had not even set foot on Flannan soil.

The sound of clashing blades came from the deck, screams and the slashing of flesh ... then it stopped. Alexander waited, not daring to breathe in case a crazed crew member came to kill him as well.

Tenpin, covered in red, slammed through the door, and without a word, grabbed Alexander and rushed onto the deck, past the dead bodies, all twenty of them, and threw Alexander into the sea. Alexander's last thoughts blurred in seconds, but he knew, if he could hold onto details, he might be able to piece together all he could.

Growsly's body, he had seen that, and nineteen others. As his body flew into the sea, he thought, twenty-three people on board, twenty dead ... Tenpin and I survived ... who was the other? Alexander plunged into the open sea.

Green and blue. Sinking and reaching. The world was pulling and pushing itself, and one side was winning. Reality grew smaller, light began to disappear from sight. Alexander's lungs were full. He had struggled, but he had now given up. He was fully capable of letting himself die.

His teacher had taught him he was not necessary

... that he would die when his time came, that that was natural, a way of life ... but what else? The Master had said something else ... what had followed? His mind travelled back to the last day he had seen his master.

"Yes, Master? You wanted to speak with me," said Alexander with a newfound strength and determination that he would never have even dreamt of had he remained on the street.

"Not speak with you, speak to you." The Master turned on his chair to face the boy. "One last thing I must tell you before we part ways."

Alexander was shocked. "What? Part ways?" He was horrified. His master, his teacher, was leaving him. "I can't live on my own!"

The Master grinned. "Please ... just listen."

Alexander sat, unease sitting in the pit of his stomach.

"In the past, we have spoken of philosophy, biology and botany, society, we have explored techniques and skills of all kinds ... but beyond all of these things there is greater knowledge. Understanding of why everything is the way it is, it is known as, omniscience. Knowledge and comprehension unending."

Alexander pondered. "What does this have to do with me? And what of us parting ways?"

Once more the Master grinned. "When I was a boy, my mind was opened to this knowledge and understanding."

Alexander's eyes opened until the sockets could no longer be seen. "You were gifted knowledge of gods?"

The Master stroked his long white beard. "Gifted ...." He looked distant, and Alexander wondered why.

"So what should I do, please, go on."

The Master raised from his chair. "Now you must listen, and speak not in return." He continued, gesturing to the map on the wall. "Flannan Isle is where you must go, there you will meet the question that will make things clear to you. Take all the knowledge I have given you, and take this, it's a package that you will need for the journey; however, only open it when you must."

Alexander took the package and placed it into his bag, forgetting about it instantly.

"There are men setting sail for Flannan Isle as we speak. The harbour, there you must go, now, before the ship leaves."

Alexander rose from his chair, sadness in his eyes; he walked to the door.

"And Alexander!" the Master bellowed. "Never ... ever ... give up."

Alexander pushed himself to the shore with all the strength he had left. But it wouldn't matter, because he could feel that he would die before the sun even had the chance to set. He was frozen to the bone, and his clothes were soaked in seawater. Once more, he was prepared to die, but, suddenly, he felt a great warmth from inside himself. Where had it come from? He didn't know, but it gave him the strength to move on.

Alexander climbed the rocky slope up to the lighthouse, stumbling along the grassy plain towards the high standing stick of white. "Jaress goin hadaf," came a booming voice; Alexander fell in shock, the island grew in size, it seemed to pulsate in the presence of the voice, and follow its every command.

"What! Who's there?" screamed the exhausted, but determined Alexander, forcing himself to stand. It began to rain, and the clouds thundered overhead. Mud formed instantly; Alexander slipped and fell many times. Each time, however, he stood once more, pressing on against the wind and hail, ignoring the booming thunder and scorching lightning. When he slipped, give up he did not. Yes ... he would die, but never, ever... if he could do anything about it. In that moment, he threw away all fear.

"Loo jarah tami koma," the voice persisted in its efforts to test Alexander's strength. Such power he could hear in its voice. But the Master had taught him that fear was an enemy that held more strength then the opponent itself. He stomped on through the mud and dirt, forces unknown pushed and pulled at Alexander body, he bled from the pressure, and was deafened by the sounds and high pitched noises that surrounded him.

This was certainly a test, for if he was intended to be killed, by now, he would be, he knew that. Alexander knew that he could make it to the lighthouse, more of a candle now; it shrunk ten inches for every single inch he moved forward. He gathered all his lasting strength and reached for the lighthouse door. It was not as he expected. When he opened it, the lighthouse was gone, as was Flannan Isle, and everything, it seemed. Alexander could not comprehend where he was, or ... anything. It was empty.

Alexander swum in the nothingness, twisting, or turning, or some sickening combination of both.

"Hello," came a surreal presence.

"Hi," came Alexander's voice.

"What is your name?" The presence flowed, almost, everywhere, across all of time and all of space ... or so it seemed. That was how Alexander felt it. But ... the thing was, he didn't really know at all. Could he even hear a voice. A voice? He was confused.

"I don't know."

"You are ... a boy?"

"Yes ... I think so..." said the boy.

"Am I a boy?" flowed the presence, as its movements seemed to ask.

"Is everything a boy?" asked the boy in return.

"To some degree," smiled the presence. "The opposite is its opposite without its concentration of opposition."

He knew of this idea.

"What of events? Surely some things are factual?" inquired the boy.

"Did I say they weren't?" flowed the presence.

"But if everything is everything, what is true? What can be considered fact if everything is everything and nothing?"

"Fact is made factual by your perceptions."

"But only if you believe that is so," the boy stated proudly.

The presence smiled. "You are wise for a ...."

"Yes, I was going to ask, what am I?" He stood waiting; he received no direct answer. The boy could not see anything; he felt, smelt and heard only what the Presence wished him to sense, everything else was just nothing. He couldn't even perceive himself; he was an idea, a million concepts floating inside a blank box, and there were others there.

The boy could sense thousands of others around him, screaming, their faces forming endless voids of desperation and fear. All these people, were they the many men who had disappeared near the mysterious lighthouse? Was this the prison of all those foolish enough to come to Flannan Isle?

Suddenly, he was approached ... or was given, perhaps both, by a flooding of knowledge. Flannan Isle is home to a number of ... gods, or rather, 'higher beings' that researched the mortal plane of existence ... to see if mortals could ever have the knowledge of their species ... to test them. The Master was given omniscience, but not free will; he has been controlled by these beings, to teach other mortals in the ways of mortality, and then was tasked with sending them to Flannan Isle, to be tested by their species.

The ship ... yes, it was indeed very old ... forever sailing the passage of time, sailing the students of the Master to Flannan Isle since the day the old man first visited Flannan Isle, all those centuries ago. The boy was given a vision from the Presence, of the Master and of Captain Tenpin, outside, trying to breach the lighthouse.

"One day, the Master, through his growing knowledge, began to overpower our will; today is the day that he has finally found the strength to combat us; he comes now, with the one you call Tenpin."

The Presence continued to tell the boy everything. But why would the Presence tell him any of this? Why give a mortal knowledge of their presence here? Suddenly, the Master and Captain Tenpin entered the Nothingness that was home to the Higher Beings.

"I have waited many years for this day," said the Master.

The Presence went still, all was silent, the Master raised his hands, and the Presence began to twist and shake uncontrollably. The Presence screamed in agony as the Nothingness began to tear apart; the Master was destroying them, the Higher Beings were being destroyed by his power.

Tenpin stared in astonishment, as did Alexander, as the Higher Beings were crushed and shrivelled away, the lighthouse began to reappear, and Alexander could feel hope. The Master had saved him again.

Tenpin and Alexander smiled as the last of the Nothingness disappeared. The Master smiled too; the Higher Beings were destroyed, never again would they conduct sick experiments on mortals. But suddenly, the Master held his stomach in pain, as he was torn apart by an unknown force.

They were still there, they had fooled the mortals. Tenpin was gone, vanished from sight, only Alexander was left, at the base of the lighthouse. The sun had set and it was dark. Alexander knew not what to do, until a voice in his head spoke to him.

Extinguish the flame at the lighthouse's head, that is their heart, destroy it. Alexander could not tell who had given him this information, and knew it could be a trap, but he had no other choice; he climbed the stairs, running as fast as he could without falling, and reached the lighthouses peak.

A great beacon was alight at the lighthouse's tip, it was magnificent, truly holy and a remarkable sight to behold. But Alexander knew that it must be destroyed. He stepped forward, his mind prepared to do whatever necessary to destroy these beings. The ones who had killed the only father he had ever known. Such hatred he had within him as he leapt towards the beacon. As he struck, his mind was full of fury, but his body was not his own; he was still and could not move. Alexander had no control over himself. Once again, the beings had him, and this time, the Master could not save him.

"You disgust me!" Alexander spat.

The beings laughed. "You know nothing child." They sang in unison, "You are ours, we made you." They chanted.

Alexander struggled. "Your tricks will not work on me!"

"They are not tricks child ... you killed your master, not us, it was you. He was perfectly capable of striking us down. But you destroyed him. You did not know it, but you did. That ... is how we made you."

Alexander was appalled by their words, and began to cry and curse. "No! This cannot be!"

"Oh, but it is, youngling. We saw the strength the old man had gained. We had to act, so we created you, he trusted you, and we used that. Don't you see? Love, compassion, trust and loyalty, they are nothing! They are weaknesses, and that is why your species will never be as powerful as we are."

Alexander's head bowed, overwhelmed, and exhausted. "Please." he panted, the life leaving his eyes.

The Higher Beings erupted in laughter, and their booming voices filled the ears of every person for miles around. "You mortals are pathetic."

"We ... are ... all ... we can be ... at ... this ... time ... in our ... evolution ..."

The beings had tired of their games. "We will destroy you now."

Alexander thought of his life up until now ... did it all mean nothing? Everything the Master had taught him? Wait ... he thought ... the Master ... "Before you do ..." began Alexander, "how did you do it? Outsmart the Master? Surely you must be grand to defeat one with knowledge equal to yours." Alexander played with their egos.

"Well ... yes, but it is to be expected ... we are, after all, IMMORTAL!" The Higher Beings began to chatter amongst themselves. At first, they spoke of THEM, as a united brilliance. Alexander listened, waiting ... eventually, one of them spoke as an individual. "Indeed, boy, we are powerful beyond imagining."

Alexander smirked. "Oh ... so you are the leader? Greater than the others?"

The Higher Beings protested.

"No ... of course not." said the individual.

"Then why do you speak for the others? I think you believe yourself better than them."

There was uproar amongst the Higher Beings. There were great explosions and booming waves of verbal abuse as they fought amongst themselves; at first, they all fought the individual, but it began to go beyond that. They began to claim leadership, and piece by piece, the restraints on Alexander loosened. He reached for his bag; from within it, he drew the package the Master had given him. He opened it; flashing light came from within it, and filled Alexander's sight.

Once again, Alexander's mind was overcome by vision; he was in the mind of the Master. He felt his thoughts. The Master had been trapped by the Higher Beings for hundreds of years. He had finally found the power to overthrow them. But he needed to be certain that his plan would work. After thinking it over for years, he came to a conclusion. He had to die, it was the only way he would fool the Higher Beings. So every night, he used his knowledge to place, piece by piece, the power that was necessary to destroy the Higher Beings, into Alexander's mind.

Alexander released himself from his bonds and unleashed the power within him into the minds of the squabbling Higher Beings. It was too much for them. They saw a young boy with his parents by the river collecting berries. They felt the love that the parents had for their son, and the joy in the heart of the child. Their minds were torn by mortal emotion, the pain in the heart of the boy that stood before them. The longing for love and care, and the pain that came from the loss of his only friend, the Master.

It was in that moment that the Higher Beings were destroyed, forever to be trapped in the mind of an orphan child. The will of the Master flowed across the lands, love and compassion rose in the hearts of every child, man and woman around the world.

Captain Tenpin was a child once more; he was with

his parents again, and every time they asked what he wanted, he laughed and jumped into their arms. Their family donated their fortune to the local orphanage.

Growsly was at school once more, but this time, he was not bullied and rejected, he was embraced, and had friends and grew up to be the leader of his local council.

The Master was gone, but his message lived on. You might ask what happened to Alexander. No one really knows, but some say, when you sail past Flannan Isle, you can still hear the laughter of a child and his parents, by the river, picking berries.

The figure gives the animal pelt to the shopkeeper.

NOT ONE BEING THAT HAS ever lived has never been hopeless. No person has ever gone on without giving up: at least for a time. Nothing has happened without a consequence. But nothing is not a consequence. Does this mean nobody is free? But we are not restrained. No invisible hand guides us; no unknown mind controls our thoughts. We have freedom in the sense that we can make our own choices. Choices. Freedom. Hope. Interlacing ideas in that we look for a pattern; we need a pattern. Everything must link. Reality? Beauty ... but beauty is in the eye of the beholder; this we know. Paint the man, cut the lines. Paint The Man, Cut The Lines. No, he whines, please, I'm innocent. PAINT THE MAN, CUT THE LINES. I have to shout over his screams. But eventually they die down. Hush ... Now you sleep ...

This is beauty. All colour, a mirage of perfection.

Depictions of men, women, beasts. Poetry, imagination carries what the words cannot. But they do, for the writer knows a mind will read these words. A vast world, everything working together without knowing, for they want for themselves. But they save everything around them by their sacrifices, by their way. They do not mean to do what they do, but they save more than themselves by doing it.

This is beauty. Does anything exist but our world? Distant glimmering points in the sky. Though we see hope, though we see beauty, though we see freedom ... they see nothing. The Universe doesn't care. In life you learn, sooner or later, that some people care about everything, and some, nothing. And those who care about nothing have nothing care about them. And those who care about everything have nothing that cares about them.

Nothing, except themselves.

I had a nightmare.

That loyalty was a precursor to a knife in the back.

That heroes murdered the innocent for breadcrumbs.

That war was smiled upon as if a game.

That justice was only for whoever had the most money.

That those who cared for anything but themselves were dying.

That a man is nothing but the sum of his memories.

That everything we do has a consequence ...

But it means nothing.

And when I opened my eyes ...

It was much the same.

Free will doesn't exist. Everything is the product of cause and effect. Even a belief that contradicts this. I am wrong. I am wrong. It's all just values and numbers:

```
OIOIOIOOOIIIOOIOOIIIOIOIOIIIOIOOOIIOIOOOOOIOOOO
OOIIOIOOIOIIIOOIIOOIOOOOOOIIIOIIIOIIOIOOOOIIOOO
OIOIIIOIOOOOIOOOOOIIIOIIIOIIOOIOIOOIOOOOOOIIOO
OOIOIIOIIOOOIIOIIOOOOIOOOOOOIIOOOIOOIIOOIOIOIIO
IIOOOIIOIOOIOIIOOIOIOIIIOIIOOIIOOIOIOOIOIIIOOOIOO
OOOOOOOIIOIOOOOIOIOOIOOOOOIOIIOIIIOOIIOOIOOOOI
OOOOOOIIIOIIIOIIOOIOIOOIOOOOOOIIOOOIOOIIOOIOIOI
IOIIOOOIIOIOOIOIIOOIOIOIIIOIIOOIIOOIOIOOIOOOOOOI
IOOIOIOIIIOIIOOIIOOIOIOIIOOIOOIIIOOIOIIIOIOOOIIO
IOOOOIIOIOOIOIIOIIIOOIIOOIIIOOIOOOOOOIIOIOOIOIII
OOIIOOIOOOOOIIOOIOOOIIOOOOIOIIIOOIOOIIOIOIIOII
OOIOIOIIIOOIOOIOOOOOOIIIOIIIOIIOIOOOOIIOOIOIOII
OIIIOOOIOOOOOIIIOIIIOIIOOIOIOOIOOOOOOIIOIOOOOI
IOOOOIOIIIOIIOOIIOOIOIOOIOOOOOOIIOIIIOOIIOIIIIOOI
OOOOOOIIOIOOOOIIOIIIIOIIIOOOOOIIOOIOIOIOOIOIIIOOO
OOIIOIOOOOIOIOOIOOOOOIOIIOIIIOOIIOOIOOOOIOOOOO
OIIIOOOOOIIOIIIIOIIOIIIOOIIOOIOOOIIOOIOIOIIIOOIOO
IIOIOOIOIIOIIIOOIIOOIIIOOIOOOOOOIIIOIO.
```

Are we seeing more of the Voices that Opaulde introduced earlier on? Have different parts of Opaulde invented these stories and expressed these thoughts? Who is Opaulde?

—Darcy

Chapter Seven

IT IS ... 'THE LITTLE THINGS'. Little actions, reactions, occurrences and thoughts. Building on each other. Again. And again. For an infinite number of times. That has always equaled the sum of everything. That is the simplest understanding of reality-from-within-our-minds I believe we can have. Yet often I hear words that echo: "Nothing I do will make a difference." But that ... is the greatest lie we can tell ourselves. For EVERYTHING makes a difference. It is in this that we find our greatest threat ... and our greatest tool. This is reality ... as much as we can completely understand it. Reality outside of our minds is something we can taste ... but is that in itself just another illusion?

I speak these words as if I am a master of the Universe. I speak them as if I have any sort of control over my reality. I speak them like a frightened child yelling out into the ni—

ARGH!

Voices ...

Images ...

Steps ...

NO!

Eyes of crystal soften my haunted mind like the slow ebbing of an ocean tide.

Strands of purity flow into my soul, and make it seem good to be alive ...

And ...

Human ...

LIES!

DON'T LISTEN!

Who are you? Why are you so distressed? What are you doing inside my mind?

PLEASE! HELP ... Help.

I want to. But you have to—

ARGH!

ARGH!

LIES!

Memories fall upon my face like distant relatives sending greetings from far ... far away.

Dreams dance across fields and sing of times of merriment and celebration.

My stomach is full. And the warm touch of my companion makes it seem good to be alive. And ... hum.

NO.

Grace is no longer with me. That was sudden, indeed,

much like the changes in everything that I have written. The so called 'twists and turns'.

The dynamic of life.

From Blair to Grace, I have speculated from a variety of emotional states. I have been arrogant, I have been witty, I have been distraught and I have been sadistic. I have made many mistakes and I may make many more.

We are beings of emotion. We feel. That is no more special than the way a rock is a rock. Ah, but speciality is relative, isn't it, and thus is a construct of emotion itself.

Everything is such. It's beautiful, disgusting and nothing. All of these things and none of them. Because they are all constructs of our adorable, pathetic, little, immense perceptions.

The dynamic of life, though, forms a flux in these things. That is the essence of adventure. Processes are the story of emotion.

Somewhere along the process, we may meet, and if we do, we will react to each other as we might and may continue on along the story.

I have, again, lost the thing that I believed would be my comfort. But each time this has happened I have, in ways, grown, and my story has led me to greater confidence and independence.

But still, I will continue, as all of us may, as long as we spend our time here:

Chasing pillows.

OIOOIIIO OIIOIIII OOIOIIIO OOIOOOOO OIOOIIIO OIIOIIII
OOIOIIIO OOIOOOOO OIOIOOOO OIIOIIOO OIIOOIOI

OIIOOOOI OIIIOOII OIIOOIOI OOIOOOOO OIIOIOOO
OIIOOIOI OIIOIIOO OIIIOOOO OOIOOOOO OIIOIIOI
OIIOOIOI OOIOIIIO OOIOOOOO OIOOIOOI OIIIOIOO
OOIOOIII OIIIOOII OOIOOOOO OIIOOOOI OOIOOOOO
OIIOIIOO OIIOIOOI OIIOOIOI OOIOIIIO OOIOOOOO
OIOIOIOO OIIOIOOO OIIOOIOI OIIIIOOI OOIOOOOO
OIIOIIOO OIIOIOOI OIIOOIOI OOIOIIIO OOIOOOOO
OIOIOIOO OIIOIOOO OIIOOIOI OIIIOOIO OIIOOIOI
OOIOIIIO OOIOIIIO OOIOIIIO.

DO YOU UNDERSTAND NOW? **W**HAT is inside my head? All of these things flow through my mind and they manifest as Voices that can't seem to ever agree with one another. Fractured thoughts. Nothing is ever complete. But perhaps, when put together ... they form an emotional web that comes close to something you could call wholeness.

Who knows. Maybe that's up to you.

I saw the moon this evening. It seemed to be falling towards Earth at an alarming speed. But no; it was merely the clouds moving across it giving the illusion that the movement was the moon. Sometimes we are deceived. Sometimes, I'm sure, we cannot understand. But that idea ... not understanding ... is as much us as anything else. Or am I wrong? Am I deceived? These thoughts go on forever. Growing in complexity until you are left with something that mimics what you have just read.

Chaos. But chaos is a human idea, as well ... so what can we believe? In the things of this world that make us 'us'. Happiness, the most prominent. Happiness is goodness. Let us strive, in short, for goodness for all. For it is possible. I no longer believe in impossibility. Just a lack of understanding. They are not the same thing. Or maybe they are. Maybe ... that's up to you.

Maybe ...

In a way.

Everything is.

We all chase our pillows. The things that comfort us. Or give us pleasure. Whatever it is we seek ... the emotional tale of our species is so very extensive. And sometimes it's easy to get lost when you are a thinker in this world. Sometimes we thinkers look at the world: at the mindless brutes, raping, destroying and descending our people into chaos. But sometimes we see beauty. Something special. I want to be special. Has all of this just been in my head? I cannot remember anymore ... what is real? Who really am I? Who really was I? What came before this?

Opaulde

TEXT WRITTEN AS SUCH: (*) is commentary on behaviour, thoughts or attitudes.

SCENE ONE

curtains closed

civilian walks onto the stage from the right, a man is sitting on a chair, reading a book

Man: Would you care to hear a story?

Civilian: Oh! (she/he is late for an appointment) I'm very sorry but I am late for an appointment! (she/he is quite off put by the man's appearance)

Man: A job interview, I know. You don't want that job. (he/she is being quite blatant, yet calm)

Civilian: How on earth do you know about that? (she/he is beginning to be concerned for her/ his own safety)

Man: If you listen to a story of mine, everything will be explained. Have you forgotten the stories your grandfather once told you when you were only little? Is there no time for a tale anymore?

Civilian: (she/he is overwhelmed) *sits in the chair next to him/her*

Man: The story of Opaulde is a very uncommon tale that I often flick back to when I am bored. I won't spoil anything for you, merely make a point of what I find so interesting about it. Opaulde was not your average child. Nor were his parents. For you see, his mother, eccentric and sometimes violent, was the one to give him his rather odd name ... Opaulde, you see. His father, a businessman, but not of the same ilk as the stereotypical office worker, craved time away from his simple existence. And so the two of them, their names unknown to history, made a family in the mountains. It was peaceful at first. But Opaulde's mother grew restless, and soon disappeared. Both of his parents died, yet Opaulde survived. There is evidence implying that the boy ate his parents.

Civilian: That's ghastly! Is this child locked up? Surely something like that doesn't leave a child with their sanity.

Man: No ... for I don't believe he even remembered it ... the investigation was inconclusive. And as for sanity ... well. He found his own form of sanity, I believe. Somewhere along the line. For don't we all? ... Find our own little way to survive?

Civilian: I'm not here for a philosophical discussion ... actually! Why am I listening to this at all?

civilian exits stage left

Man: He was adopted, in the end ...

man exits stage right

SCENE TWO

curtains open

Ben is standing, looking out across the audience with a peaceful expression on his face

Sophie enters stage right, stamps up to Ben

Sophie: Argh! Why did we adopt that child, Ben? He's driving me insane! He won't speak! He won't go to school! All he ever does is give me that expression like he's just seen something funny! THERE'S NOTHING FUNNY

ABOUT MY FACE! And then waves goodbye to me when he's just going into the next room!

Ben: He's had a hard life, Sophie. Let him heal how he needs to.

Sophie: He's been healing for four years! And what is that goop he makes every morning? He sings to it, Ben!

Ben: We made a commitment. No ... he isn't the child we were hoping for ... but he is the child that we have been blessed with.

Opaulde enters from back right

Sophie: He needs to be fixed!

Opaulde drops his digging fork

Ben and Sophie turn around

Ben: Son. Good morning. (smiles)

momentary silence

Sophie: Why do you carry that digging fork, honey? You know it's broken, right?

Opaulde picks up his digging fork and waddles over to the chair at the front of the stage, where he sits down there is a silence, Ben and Sophie exchange looks: Sophie's of frustration and Ben's of concern

Ben: Son ...

Sophie: (suddenly furious) Wait! Opaulde, did you put that chair there! That is not the right place for the chair!

Opaulde is partially oblivious

momentary pause

Sophie pulls the chair from under Opaulde and places it to the side of the stage, Opaulde falls to the floor

Ben: Sophie, that was not necessary—

Sophie discovers Opaulde's bowl filled with goop

Sophie: No! That's it! OPAULDE! WHAT IS WRONG WITH YOU? WHAT IS THIS?

Ben and Sophie argue off stage left

curtains close

SCENE THREE

civilian enters stage left, stressed, man enters stage right

Civilian: You! What are you doing here! Stay back or I really will call the police!

Man: You didn't get the job.

Civilian: No ...

Man: You don't want that job.

Civilian: It's all I had left! My last chance!

Man: No.

Civilian: Yes!

momentary silence

Man: Do you remember the story your grandfather used to tell you about love?

Civilian: That's a story for little children.

Man: Why would you teach a child something that becomes meaningless when they're older?

Civilian: (laughs) So they don't have to know what the world is really like!

civilian storms off stage right

Man: ...what the world is really like ...

Scene Four

curtains open

Opaulde is sitting centre stage

silence

a clattering noise comes from stage right

Opaulde investigates, finding a mirror; he is startled by his reflection, but slowly approaches it, communicating through gestures to his reflection, believing it is another person with another digging fork; he places his fork up against the mirror, and smiles, reaching out slowly to his reflection and touching hands with it, believing he has found a friend ... after a time, he walks away from his reflection, waving as he goes

a boy sneaks up behind Opaulde, throwing a sheet over his head, laughing as Opaulde screams and squirms underneath it; in the chaos, Opaulde stabs the boy with his digging fork, killing him

curtains close

Scene Five

civilian and man enter stage right

Civilian: You've been following me all day! Telling me these stories ... BUT NONE OF THEM MAKE SENSE! What is the point of telling me all this?

Man: Because I want you to remember.

Civilian: Remember what?

curtains open

Ben and Sophie are sitting with Opaulde

man exits stage left

Ben: Son ... you're going to be somewhere different for a while. But you will be safe there, do you understand?

Opaulde holds onto his digging fork

Sophie: You can't take that with you! Why do you even want it? It's broken, Opaulde. It's useless. It doesn't work. It can't do the job it's meant to do.

Opaulde, Ben and Sophie freeze

Civilian: I don't understand!

Man enters behind the three frozen people

Man: It's broken. It's useless. It doesn't work. It can't do the job it's meant to do.

Civilian: Okay, so he loves a broken digging fork; why are you telling me this?!

man exits centre stage

Ben: Why do you want to keep it, Opaulde?

Opaulde gestures to the broken end of the digging fork and then to his mouth but does not say anything

Ben and Sophie lead him off the stage

civilian, frustrated, walks over to the mirror and looks into it, seeming discontent in her appearance

man enters

Man: Do you remember when your grandfather would tell you the story about your reflection in the mirror?

Civilian: I'm almost getting used to you now ... yes. I remember the story. About how your reflection is someone like you in another world. More nonsense.

Man: Perhaps ... edited ... from the truth. But all good stories are.

Civilian: There's no truth in it.

Man: Ah ... but there is. Your reflection is the image of a person like you.

Civilian: You talk like my grandfather ... my reflection is just my reflection. Nothing more.

Man: It's more to me.

silence

Man: When you greet your reflection it will greet you in the same way.

man exits stage, taking out his broken digging fork

civilian reaches out and touches her reflection ... looking back to see the man is gone

curtains close

The figure went home and went to sleep.

I have read over all of this many times. I am not certain who Opaulde truly is. Is he the lovestruck teenager? Is he the gabble of philosophical voices ranting and discussing? Or is he what he depicts himself as in that last stage play ... was that his

true identity all along? Or perhaps he is the simple hunting figure, going about his life. Maybe he is all of these things. At least in his mind he was. I do not know, and perhaps no one ever will. I merely compile the things that he has written and given to me in a frenzy. I met him only for a brief time, but I felt as if I had known him for years. Perhaps I had. Perhaps we all know Opaulde. Perhaps Opaulde is best thought of as an idea rather than a person. Because while he surely had one true reality, in his mind, he was so many things at once. Isn't that what matters in the end? What we see ourselves as? While, arguably, some of the things he has said may not be true and others are indecipherable, each point of expression he has made shows a different part of his mind. Sometimes I wonder what happened to him. This last entry is the most recent thing Opaulde has written. Think of it as you will.

—Darcy

Chapter Eight

DO YOU KNOW WHY THE trees sway?

Because the wind reminds them of the voices of their dead friend trees.

And so they wave, thinking they are finally coming home.

Sometimes I dress as a tree and go out ... they fall for it because they're blind ... it makes them happy.

They are my friends. I love them.

They make me happy, too.

Sometimes I forget them... I get so absorbed... in what I think are problems.

That I forget them.

But they never forget me.

They always wait.

You write?

What are they?

OK.

I think.

I'm.

Actually...

A.

Tree.

In a human body ...

I need your help.

To get back home.

The silence between speech.

The shiver down the spines of those who believe.

And the sparkle in the eyes of those who have seen it.

The path is open to those who are too.

See.

I was right.

Beauty is in you.

I always have.

The trees.

They're so talkative tonight.

The youth coming through.

Thank you.

For helping me get back on the road to home.

I love you.

Both, perhaps.

I wouldn't be where I am without.

Choose.

Will look after you.

I promise.

They are with you.

You will know who when you no longer need to ask.

It doesn't matter that they are gone.

No, no.

It has just made us realise what we had forgotten.

Us.

We love you.

Yes.

The third picture.

It doesn't hurt.

Hello tears.

Welcome home.

It's us.

It's okay.

You're safe now.

He is not a tree. I...

Don't ... Have ... It ...

Can I come in anyway?

It's cold.

Out there.

But I don't understand why I need to do that ...

To be with you.

I don't want to. ...no ... but.

I had hope.

She.

No?

But I don't want to die.

Please.

Let me in.

All of us.

Why did you make us leave?

They keep coming back.

We just want to be back.

Open the door.

It's changed now.

Goodbye.

~ The End ~

About the Author

WILLIAM COOPER IS A STUDENT of everything that interests him. Although everything interesting doesn't always interest him (we think it may be the hormones). He likes warm toast when he has been sick and intends to expand his novel Chasing Pillows with a "somewhat sequel" that explores the protagonist's universe and may mention the protagonist himself once or twice. When he makes mistakes he almost always tries to spin them into an intended action and does this sometimes with success.

www.ingramcontent.com/pod-product-compliance
Lightning Source LLC
Chambersburg PA
CBHW060425130626
46555CB00005B/2221